PORCH

THE PORCH

THE
PORCH

MERRILEE FRANKLIN

TATE PUBLISHING
AND ENTERPRISES, LLC

The Porch
Copyright © 2014 by Merrilee Franklin. All rights reserved.

No part of this publication may be reproduced, stored in a retrieval system or transmitted in any way by any means, electronic, mechanical, photocopy, recording or otherwise without the prior permission of the author except as provided by USA copyright law.

This novel is a work of fiction. Names, descriptions, entities, and incidents included in the story are products of the author's imagination. Any resemblance to actual persons, events, and entities is entirely coincidental.

The opinions expressed by the author are not necessarily those of Tate Publishing, LLC.

Published by Tate Publishing & Enterprises, LLC
127 E. Trade Center Terrace | Mustang, Oklahoma 73064 USA
1.888.361.9473 | www.tatepublishing.com

Tate Publishing is committed to excellence in the publishing industry. The company reflects the philosophy established by the founders, based on Psalm 68:11,
"The Lord gave the word and great was the company of those who published it."

Book design copyright © 2014 by Tate Publishing, LLC. All rights reserved.
Cover design by Junriel Boquecosa
Interior design by Gram Telen
Illustrations by Rosauro Ugang

Published in the United States of America
ISBN: 978-1-63063-274-8
1. Fiction / General
2. Fiction / Coming of Age
14.04.24

"To pretend is to lose oneself in a real-life game of make believe."

DEDICATION

This book is dedicated to my wonderful husband whose vision for this story inspired me to write!

DEDICATION

AUTHOR'S NOTE

I am thankful for my childhood years that were rich with make-believe and pretend play. My past dreams and aspirations became my present realities and my future accomplishments. I continue to pray for all of the children in my life; that they experience full lives and fulfilled dreams. I thank God for parents and teachers who encourage creativity and imagination.

> If history were taught in the form of stories, it would never be forgotten.
> —Rudyard Kipling

CONTENTS

Chapter 1 *The Japanese Puzzle Box* 13
Chapter 2 *The Old House and the Porch* 19
Chapter 3 *Ten-Year-Old Natalie-2010* 25
Chapter 4 *The Porch* 36
Chapter 5 *The History of Springfield* 41
Chapter 6 *The Fourth of July 1895* 49
Chapter 7 *Ten Year Old Sara-1910* 59
Chapter 8 *"The Treasure Chest"* 68
Chapter 9 *Sara is a Nurse* 75
Chapter 10 *Sara and Robert* 81
Chapter 11 *Excitement and Despair* 85
Chapter 12 *Ten-Year-Old Matt-1932* 92
Chapter 13 *The Fourth of July 1940* 98
Chapter 14 *Sara's Adventures* 102
Chapter 15 *Matt's Adventures* 111
Chapter 16 *The Fourth of July 1945* 117
Chapter 17 *The Berlin Airlift* 122
Chapter 18 *Ten-Year-Old Jake-1953* 126
Chapter 19 *Ten-Year-Old Mike-1965* 137
Chapter 20 *The Fourth of July 1972* 142
Chapter 21 *The Accident* 147

Chapter 22 *The Fourth of July 1974* 150
Chapter 23 *The Project* 153
Chapter 24 *Mike and Donna* 158
Chapter 25 *Ten-Year-old Barry-1991* 163
Chapter 26 *Jake's Accomplishments* 168
Chapter 27 *Game Changer* 172
Chapter 28 *The Wedding* 180
Chapter 29 *The Fourth of July 2003* 184
Chapter 30 *The Mystery Unfolds–2010* 188
Chapter 31 *The Safe* 191
Chapter 32 *The Ring* 197
Chapter 33 *The Fourth of July 2010* 202
Chapter 34 *Springfield* 213

CHAPTER 1
THE JAPANESE PUZZLE BOX

"A slip of paper falls from the puzzle box as the antique dealer shows Mike how it opens."

The year was 2010 and Mike eased the silver Ford F-150 up to the curb in front of his old mission-style house. Turning off the engine, he sat for a long while, lost in deep thought. It had been a very interesting visit to the antique dealer who had helped him to open the hidden compartment of a Japanese puzzle box. This rectangular box had probably been a mystery to this family for almost one hundred years. He was so excited, as he truly believed that he would be the one to unlock the mysteries that this old house had been hiding for the same length of time. The dealer had owned several of the antique boxes throughout the years and was familiar as to how they opened. As he began to twist and turn the box, he pointed out to Mike that the box was carved with a beautiful inlaid wood design called yosegi. The designs resembled trees, mountains, and water, three common elements characteristic of this art form. The dealer also explained that the boxes were still crafted in Japan and were very expensive to own.

After fiddling with the box for what seemed like an eternity to Mike, the dealer twisted the corners and squeezed on opposite sides of the top, releasing a bottom opening of the box. A flap with a concealed hinge swung open to reveal a small secret compartment.

"Awesome! As far as I know, this is the first time that this box has been opened," Mike exclaimed.

The dealer said, "Here, let me show you how it works. There is a sequence that has to be just right or it won't open."

As he showed Mike the sequence again, they realized that an old, folded scrap of paper had fallen on the floor. Reaching at the same time, they almost bumped heads as they grabbed for the paper. Mike picked it up and unfolded it, careful not to tear it. On the paper, there were five numbers printed in a row. He noticed immediately that the handwriting looked like the script of Archibald, the home's original owner.

Mike exclaimed, "That looks like the same handwriting that I have seen on some old letters that I have at the house. It's Archibald's handwriting! He was my great-grandfather that built the old house that I live in. What are these numbers for?"

Mike and the dealer discussed possible answers to his question and he had closed and opened the box several times so that when he got home, he would be able to show the rest of the family how it worked.

Mike had been pondering the numbers and their meaning during the long ride home. He thought out loud, "Who had the box belonged to? What were the numbers for? What will we do with them?"

He even caught himself answering his own questions with questions. "If the box belonged to Archie (Archibald's nickname) and he knew that the numbers might not be found for many years, what are we supposed to do with them now?"

He remembered looking at the box many times while he was growing up. All of the family's memorabilia would be laid out for the annual Fourth of July family reunions. On the porch of the old house, tables were draped with red, white, and blue bunting for the get-togethers and the family members would add new items and discuss the old items, teaching the younger children all about the history of the family. Mike thought that he knew all about everything, from the postcards and coins to the letters and stamps from foreign countries. He vaguely remembered his father telling him that there was something mysterious about this item. It had beautiful inlaid woodcarvings and was probably a souvenir from a trip that was taken a long time ago. At the reunions, everyone would hold it and rotate it in their hands, as if to unlock the mystery that it was sure to hold. The family always assumed that great-grandfather Archibald had put the ornate box in the "Treasure Chest." They all knew that it was old and just thought that it was something special from his past.

Mike had spent the last two years compiling information and putting together the genealogy of the family. He had researched back to 1890, when Archibald and his wife, Jewell, met, married, and moved to Springfield. Together, they had traveled, studied, and learned about the trends of architecture that were the newest fad to sweep the nation. This house with the beautiful porch had been their dream, come true.

The house had been a part of the family ever since. Mike and his wife, Donna, were now living there with their son, Barry, daughter-in-law, Cynthia, granddaughter, Natalie, and grandson, Jason. The house and the porch had withstood many harsh winters, beautiful springs and autumns, outstanding summers, and witnessed many monumental events throughout the years. Many different loved ones called this old house their home and all of the family members had special memories of the now famous porch.

Cynthia had been a huge help with the genealogy and up until an hour ago, he thought that they were just about finished sorting out all of the details of the history of the family and the house. As he sat in the truck and contemplated the now opened box and the paper with the numbers, he knew that the puzzle was far from solved. The emotions that he felt were filling him with so much excitement. He felt like a kid again, with adventure looming on the horizon. He could not wait to tell the rest of the family all about his afternoon!

He and Cynthia had organized all of the memorabilia that had accumulated in the wooden crates that were kept under the front porch. Throughout the years, the family members referred to these crates as the Treasure Chests. In 1895, it had started out as one crate and had grown through the years to include many others. The family would add to the crates any time that they had a significant piece of memorabilia. It could be an award, a travel keepsake, postcards, letters, etc. It was similar to a time capsule except that it was opened each year at the Fourth of July family reunion. They had matched and labeled all of the keepsakes with the names of family members. They used the family tree and designed a timeline based on the journals that were kept along with the keepsakes. This Japanese puzzle box was the one odd item that just didn't seem to fit into the timeline anywhere. Now, with information about the history of the box and the paper with the five numbers, Mike felt certain that there was more work to do on the history of the house. He also needed to figure out the mystery surrounding these numbers.

He asked himself once again, "What will I do next with these numbers?"

The antique dealer had told Mike that the box could possibly be one hundred years old. He concluded that the box could have been acquired in 1910. He remembered that Archie was born in 1865 and the house was built in 1895. That meant that the Japanese puzzle box could have been added to the Treasure Chest when Archie was about forty-five years old!

He wondered out loud again, "Where would Archie have gotten this box when he was forty-five years old?" Mike would need to check the journals again to see if Archie traveled when he was that age.

"Why would great-grandfather Archibald write numbers on an old piece of paper, tuck it into a box that was almost impossible to open, and leave no directions for the future?" Maybe if he went back through all of the memorabilia, he could discover something about the numbers that he and Cynthia might have missed before.

CHAPTER 2
THE OLD HOUSE AND THE PORCH

Still sitting in the truck, Mike stared at the old house, the beautiful porch spanning across the front and around the sides. He felt very nostalgic about his life and knew that he was fortunate to live here with Donna and his son's family. He had traveled most of the United States and parts of Europe and Asia, but his favorite part of every trip was returning to this house. It felt warm and safe like an old robe or a favorite quilt.

Lately, the house and the porch had been very popular. As a child, Mike had always enjoyed drawing and sketching. Not only did he sketch the house and the porch, but he could also draw action figures, futuristic cars, and monsters, just to name a few. The artwork was priceless to him, because the other guys in his class thought that he was a really good artist. It sure had been good for his self-esteem and his appetite. He was able to trade his drawings for homemade desserts that his friends' moms had packed in their lunches.

He remembered very vividly the time in the fifth grade when his teacher confiscated his spiral notebook with all of his sketches. At the end of the day, she had given them back after a stern scolding and reminder that he was not to draw during science class. Mrs. Shelton also told him that the next time she would have to send him to the office. Then she smiled slightly and quietly commented, "You are really a very good artist. I wouldn't be surprised if someday you become famous because of your drawings."

Mike remembered it as if it were yesterday. He had raced home after school on his bike and slammed the front door as he rushed in to tell his mom. "Mom, guess what? Mrs. Shelton thinks that my drawings are great and that I might be famous some day!" (He left out the part about having his notebook taken up during class.) His mom agreed with Mrs. Shelton and fixed his favorite dessert that night. He still remembered that day every time he ate cherry pie with vanilla ice cream on top.

After a long and rewarding career in developing and marketing sporting goods equipment, Mike had retired and returned to his hobby of drawing. He had been sketching comics to go along with the stories that had been handed down through the generations about his family, the house, and the porch. The stories included historical events that the family members had been a part of along with facts about famous people, ideas and inventions. The United States had experienced over one hundred years of growth during the life of this house and much of it was displayed in the memorabilia that was stored in the Treasure Chests. Mike's family, along with all Americans, had much history to teach this upcoming generation.

About a year ago, Mike had shown the comics to his friend at the local newspaper and, after seeing them, the editor of the paper called and asked to interview him. The editor wanted to print several of the comics in the newspaper along with the story of a local citizen and his retirement hobby. The rest was history. Requests poured into the paper for more of the comics and before long, newspapers around the country ran similar articles about Mike and his now famous hobby. Recently, *Not Just Any Old Porch* had become syndicated and he was getting paid to have it printed in papers around the country! Mike had even allowed himself to daydream about maybe someday winning the prestigious Rueben Award for outstanding comic illustrations.

People of all ages were reading his comics and learning about history at the same time.

Just the other day, he asked Barry and Cynthia, " Should I inquire about publishing a book with all of my comics in it? People might be interested in reading them in book format."

They chuckled as they replied, "That's a good idea. How do you plan on squeezing a few more hours out of each day to work on that project?" Silently they wondered how he did all that he did with his busy schedule. Retirement was definitely not about watching TV and taking naps.

Not Just Any Old Porch became increasingly more popular and people traveled from miles away to Springfield, to see the house and the porch. Every time that Mike noticed someone outside, he would go out to visit and invite him or her to have a glass of iced tea on the porch. He loved the notoriety that the porch was receiving and thoroughly enjoyed meeting new people. Everyone wanted to compare the drawings in the paper to the actual place where it had all happened. Along with the history of the house, the comics featured the children that had lived in the house and had played and pretended about their futures on the porch. The visitors enjoyed hearing stories first-hand and Mike never tired of reminiscing about his family.. The conversation usually included everyone comparing stories about what they had wanted to do when they 'grew up' and what they had really ended up doing in life.

Mike was so deep in thought that as he gathered his things and eased out of the truck he was surprised to see his granddaughter lying on her stomach, on the porch. She had been there the entire time that he had been sitting out front. Natalie was concentrating intently on what she was doing and hadn't even looked up when he had driven up and parked. As long as he could remember, the porch had been her favorite place to play and pretend-funny how life seemed to constantly repeat itself. Lately, as he had been filling in some of the gaps of his family history and working on the family tree, he had realized that every generation had had at least one child to live in the house, pretend, and imagine their future on the porch. The make-

The Porch

believe had included nursing, flying planes, the quest for knowledge, surfing, football plans, and now again, nursing. For the most part, the children had fulfilled their dreams, but it had not always been easy or quite the way they had imagined.

Mike had put a lot of time into thinking about childhood and how complicated it was. There was so much playing, pretending, and daydreaming; wondering how life was going to be and how the dreams were going to unfold. There had even been times in his own life when he wished that time could just freeze and stay the same. He was very nostalgic about his skateboarding years with his cousin Brandon. They had played on this very porch for hours at a time. They had pretended that their skateboards were surfboards. They perfected their balance, form, their pop-ups, and snaps and used his older brother Jake's handicap ramp to soar off of the porch and down the sidewalk. They constantly challenged each other as they planned to surf their way around the world and land the best waves on as many beaches as possible.

One memory was very vivid in his mind. He and Brandon had actually argued and fought about which of them was the best surfer. Brandon had started it one afternoon when he kept laughing at Mike's tricks. "You look like such a dork when you flip your legs around. Your arms flap out to the side and then up in the air. Looks like you're trying to fly! Fly bird, fly bird, fly!"

Mike got embarrassed and red in the face and tripped Brandon on his next run. Brandon wiped out big time and was airborne for what seemed like forever.

When he landed, he was startled and it was all he could do not to cry. As he stood up and brushed himself off, Mike whooped and hollered and rolled on the ground with uncontrollable laughter. "Now look who's flying!" Mike sputtered with sweet revenge. "That's what you get for calling me a dork." He picked up his skateboard and went in for dinner, leaving Brandon standing alone on the steps, blood dripping down his chin.

When his parents found out about it the next day, Mike was in big trouble. He had been grounded for two weeks because Brandon had a black eye and a busted lip. Everyone at school had laughed about the story, making fun of both of them. They had nicknames for a while, Bird and Bird's Cousin.

The saddest part of the memory was what he had said to Brandon in his fit of anger. "If I'm not the best surfer in the world, then I hope we don't ever surf around the world together." Little did he know that those words would haunt him for the rest of his life. Weeks later, they were back to being best friends as if nothing had ever happened. Oh, to be ten years old again, lost in a real-life game of make believe.

CHAPTER 3
TEN-YEAR-OLD NATALIE-2010

"As Mike returns home, he finds Natalie pretending to nurse her young patients on the porch."

Natalie now realized that her granddaddy Mike was out front and she looked up as he was getting out of the truck.

She hollered, "Hi, Granddaddy!"

He responded by calling back to her, "Natalie, what are you playing today?"

She laughed her sweet little laugh, knowing that he already knew the answer to that question. "Nurse, of course," Natalie replied.

He was at the foot of the steps by now and he teasingly asked her, "Did you help all of your patients to feel better? Did they have a good day?"

Her face turned solemn as she replied, "I've done my best, but some of the kids are not doing so well today. They are really sick from their treatments. One of the little boys had to be put back on the dialysis machine. His kidneys are shutting down and his parents are going to spend the night with him tonight. I don't know if he is going to make it."

She wanted to be a nurse for children with cancer and were in the hospital undergoing treatments. Her desire in life was to try to ease the suffering of the little children and bring smiles to their faces even when they were facing uncertainty and pain. In the evenings, after her homework was done, Natalie would do research on the computer. She wanted to learn all that she could about different types of cancer and the different treatments that were used to treat them. There was new information almost daily and she hungered for as much knowledge as she could find. She also learned that she needed to study psychology so that she would be able to say the most comforting words and be the right type of person in each situation. Most of her friends didn't know what they wanted to be when they grew up. They spent their free time on the computer with their Webkinz or at the TV with video games. Natalie was sure that being a nurse was what she wanted to do.

Natalie had become interested in cancer treatment research after her best friend at school in the second grade had died from cancer. It had been a rough time for her as she tried to understand why disease affected children. She had gone to a counselor for a while, but she still had so many questions about illness and dying. The experience had left Natalie even more determined that she wanted to help children and families that were dealing with cancer-type diseases.

Her parents constantly encouraged her to bring a friend home from school or to invite someone over to play on the weekends. She had finally found a new friend at school whose name was Erin. It would never be the same as it was with Charlotte, but Natalie was ready to try again. Erin went to daycare after school and her parents were divorced. On the weekends, she was usually at her dad's apartment that was in a suburb about thirty minutes away. She and her mom lived with her mom's parents in a small house that was across town from where Natalie lived. It was hard to find a time when Erin could come over to play.

They were what the other kids at school called loners. They were quiet, good students and got teased a lot about being the teacher's pets. Natalie and Erin only played games with others when they had to during PE. They would spend recess walking around the playground talking or maybe swinging if the swings were not too crowded. Erin listened politely as Natalie recounted her make-believe conversations with her patients and their parents and Erin told Natalie all about the horses that she loved to ride at the stables near her dad's apartment. Natalie always asked about Erin's weekends with her dad and secretly wondered what it was like to have divorced parents and two houses.

Natalie did invite Erin to come over to play one afternoon after school. After a snack in the kitchen, she got all of her dolls and hospital beds set up on the porch.

She suggested, "Why don't we pretend that all of our patients have the Swine Flu? They are here at the hospital because they have breathing problems and we need to make sure that they each have a treatment with a breathing machine and take their medications."

Erin agreed, but even though she had contracted the H1N1 strain of the flu six months earlier, she replied, "I don't know what you want me to do." Natalie suggested, Why don't you pretend to check the children's temperatures and monitor their oxygen levels."

Once again, Erin had trouble and seemed uncomfortable with this kind of make-believe. Natalie tried something different. She said, "Erin, would you please record the vitals that I am going to call out? Use the chart on this clipboard and fill in the data next to each patient's name."

Erin cooperated for a while and finally said, "Natalie, I don't want to hurt your feelings, but I'm bored. I don't know why you think that this is so much fun. This is really kind of depressing, taking care of sick children. What do you do if one of them dies?"

Natalie thought about defending her love for nursing, but instead got real quiet and quickly put everything away. Erin knew that she had hurt Natalie's feelings and tried to apologize several more times. After the porch was cleaned up, they decided to watch some television together until it was time for Erin's mother to pick her up. It had been an awkward afternoon and Natalie didn't think that Erin would want to come over again anytime soon.

    Erin loved horses and talked about them incessantly. One Saturday afternoon, she invited Natalie to go with her to the stables where she kept her horse. Erin showed Natalie how she groomed him and cleaned his stall. They saddled up her horse and rented a horse for Natalie to ride. It was fun to try something new, but after a while, Natalie could only think about how sore her back and legs were getting. She ended up wishing that she could go home to her porch and play nurse with her patients. She realized that the two of them had similar personalities, but very different interests. Natalie was glad that Erin was her friend even though they had different ways that they wanted to spend their free time.

    Now, when they strolled around the outskirts of the playground the conversations were about other topics. "Natalie, are you going to try out for choir?" Erin asked one day.

    "I don't want to, are you?" Natalie replied.

    "I don't know, I really don't want to get up early to come to the extra rehearsals and I'm nervous about standing up on the stage in front of everyone at the program."

    Natalie reasoned, "My parents think that I need to be involved in something extra at school. Maybe we should. I will, if you will." They walked in silence for a while knowing that they would probably try out for choir and if they both made it, they would have something to do together.

Natalie was also thinking about a news story that she had seen recently. A singing celebrity had been visiting a Children's Hospital. She had been singing lullabies to the small children and had played her guitar with some of the older children. The news commentator had mentioned that hospitals were realizing the importance of music as a therapy for ailing children. Natalie wanted to know everything there was to know about all of the aspects of nursing and thought that she might need to know more about music.

The afternoon that Mike had been to the antique dealer, Natalie had used an empty oatmeal box to construct an MRI scanning unit. With the lid off, she cut off the closed end and wrapped construction paper around it in order to cover up the writing. She was using the stretcher out of her doctor and nurse kit and was guiding it through the cylinder. Natalie was trying to determine where the cancer was in her patient's brain and if it had spread to any other parts of his body. She had carefully dressed her young patient in a drape made out of a paper towel and reassured him as she pretended to start the test. She spoke with a soft, consoling voice, "It will be noisy and clanky-sounding, but you must lie very still. We have these earphones so that you can listen to your favorite music while we run the test. If at any time, you need me, just talk out loud and I will be able to talk back to you. The test will be over with before you know it."

She had studied different types of cancer in children and knew that she could probably become a doctor, but her real desire was to be a nurse. She knew that nurses were able to spend more time with the patients and she related so well with little children. She had been able to help some of her neighbors with their toddlers. Even though she was shy with children her own age, she liked playing and caring for younger kids.

She read on the Internet about a new field of study for hospital workers. You combined degrees in nursing, teaching, and psychology in order to care for young cancer patients that needed to stay in the hospital for long periods of time. This type of a nurse would be able to teach the children and their families about their disease and at the same time occupy the many hours of each day with crafts and activities. The time would go faster for them and their minds would not be focusing on their pain and treatments. Natalie loved to do all of these things and knew that this would be an interesting and challenging career for her. She had just about finished up with her pretend patient when granddaddy Mike came up the steps to the porch. Natalie noticed the Japanese puzzle box in his hand.

"Granddaddy, did you take the puzzle box to the antique dealer?"

Mike answered, guardedly, "I did."

"Well, what did you find out?" Natalie's voice was impatient. "You know that I wanted to go with you."

Mike carefully worded his response so that he wouldn't hurt her feelings. "I had to make an appointment and the only openings they had were during school hours."

"Oh," Natalie responded, "I guess that's okay. Did you get the box opened?"

"I did, but I would love to tell the entire story this evening at the dinner table. Would you be okay with that?"

"But..." Natalie began to object, as they were interrupted.

Jason, Natalie's younger brother, raced up the sidewalk, bolted the steps two at a time and rushed by the both of them. He slammed through the front door. "Mom, where are you?" Jason hollered.

Natalie and Granddaddy Mike looked at each other, both thinking the same thing. Jason would usually stop and hug his granddaddy and almost always stopped to make fun of Natalie and her pretend hospital. They knew at once that something must be wrong.

They followed Jason into the kitchen where he began to rinse his arm off under the cold water. On her way in, Natalie reminded Jason, "Mom's gone to the store."

Granddaddy and Natalie saw blood, but didn't panic.

Jason looked up at them and calmly stated, "I'm okay. I was at the park with my friends and fell against the slide on the fort. There was a sharp place on the railing that I cut my arm on."

Natalie went to get clean cloths and peroxide, a few bandages, some salve, and some gauze. Granddaddy continued to help Jason rinse his arm and put pressure on the cut. It didn't appear to need stitches and best he could remember, Jason had had a tetanus shot the last time that he gotten hurt, which was about six weeks ago. Natalie returned and began to nurse Jason's arm. Granddaddy stepped back and allowed her to take control of the situation. She toweled his arm dry and then poured the peroxide on the cut, allowing it to bubble for a while. After drying it again, she examined the wound. It seemed clean so she applied some antibiotic ointment. Natalie had been explaining each step of the process to Jason and now stated, "I think that a butterfly bandage is all that you'll need. It will keep the cut closed so that it'll heal without much of a scar. We'll wrap it with this gauze so that it stays clean and dry." Her mannerisms were very soothing and her voice remained steady and relaxed as she nursed his wound.

She thought to herself, *I'm really good at this and I'm so glad that the sight of blood and bruised skin doesn't make me queasy.*

When they were finished, Jason decided that he had played enough for one day and went to lie on the couch and play his video game until it was time for supper.

As Natalie and Granddaddy Mike cleaned up the sink area, Mike commented to Natalie, "I'm very proud of you. You handled that very well and helped Jason to stay calm. You seemed to know exactly what to do. I am always so amazed that you are so mature for your age."

"Thank you granddaddy," replied Natalie, "I love playing nurse, but more than anything, I love to help real people instead of my pretend patients."

As Natalie and granddaddy cleaned up the towels and blood in the kitchen, Jason could hear parts of what they were saying. His arm was really throbbing. Even though he had gotten to Level 7 on his new game, he had a hard time concentrating and decided not to play anymore. He thought about the way in which his sister had taken care of his arm. Jason also thought about how many times he had messed up her play hospital on the porch or teased her about playing nurse. He was starting to realize that she was really good at this nursing thing. He wondered for a brief second if she would really be a nurse when she grew up.

At dinner that evening, Barry, Cynthia, Mike, Donna, Natalie, and Jason were all seated at the table. Mike recounted the story of the afternoon at the antique dealer's store. They had barely raised their heads from their prayer when Natalie started in. "Granddaddy took the Japanese puzzle box to the antique dealer today without me, but I think that he knows something that he isn't telling."

Mike smiled at her precocious personality and said, "I told you why I had to go when I did."

"Never mind with all of that," Cynthia interrupted their banter, "What did you find out?"

Mike hastily responded, "The dealer showed me how to open the box, it is really quite simple. I have practiced lots of times and I will teach each of you, one at a time."

"So, is it worth a bunch of money? Aren't old things usually worth a lot?" Jason asked, almost choking on a mouthful of food.

"Son, please don't talk with your mouth full." Barry corrected. "It's rude and you might choke. Apparently,

Natalie has had to nurse you once already today. Let's not go for two times."

"Sorry, Dad," Jason replied, thinking about the fact that his arm was still throbbing.

Mike continued to tell about his findings. "As the dealer opened the puzzle box, a slip of paper with numbers on it, fell to the floor."

Natalie interrupted and exclaimed, "That is neat! It's like a mystery. Can we see?"

"Right after dinner," Mike replied.

Cynthia added, "Right after all your homework is done and you kids are ready for bed."

Before bed, Mike took time to show each one, the sequence of twists and turns needed to open the box and the slip of paper that had fallen out of it. They all speculated about the paper, but there were many questions that no one really knew the answers to.

CHAPTER 4
THE PORCH

Later that evening, Mike was sitting alone, in the dark, on the front porch. The weather was cool and crisp and the sky was full of stars. There was enough moonlight for Mike to see the features of the house and the porch. As he studied the porch, he thought about Natalie and how she had gone from one moment of playing nurse, in her own world of make-believe, to the next moment of real life, helping with her brother's cut arm.

He remembered the many hours that he had spent on the porch, caught up in his own world of pretend. He and his cousin Brandon had been inseparable and would collapse with exhaustion, right here after hours of skateboarding. He also remembered an afternoon when he had come home with his arm hurting and bleeding. He had not been as lucky as Jason was this afternoon. He didn't have a sister to help nurse him and comfort him and his arm had been broken.

For the next six weeks he and Brandon had found other things to do in the afternoons and when Mike

The Porch

was alone, he had begun to draw and sketch. He would sketch action heroes and futuristic cars. He would sketch airplanes and monsters. He also sketched this house and the now famous porch. He had actually saved some of those sketches in the Treasure Chests. At the time, he thought that it was silly to put them in there with so much important stuff, but now, he was glad that they had been saved. He was actually able to use some of them in his new comic series that he was drawing. He wondered, *What if some day, those early sketches are worth a lot of money?*

He remembered the symmetry of the front of the house as he would draw. There were wide concrete steps in the middle and the four columns of brick, two on each side. As you walked up the steps, the front door was in the middle with a large window on each side. The windows were tall and came almost down to the floor of the porch. He figured that this was for air circulation before the time of air conditioning. The windows could be opened to let the breeze move throughout the house. Above the front door was a section of stained glass that had been ordered from New York and he remembered reading about it in some of the information in the Treasure Chests. In the past, the window had been blown out by a storm and had been repaired. Part of the glass that had been replaced had been kept in the Treasure Chests. When he was a teenager, they had gotten a new front door and his parents had tried to purchase one that was as close of a match as possible to the original one. Next to the front door was the original doorbell. It was not wired to ring like a modern doorbell, because when the house was built, it only had electricity to the major parts of the house. The bell was similar to the type that you might have on a tricycle or a bicycle.

After sketching the front part of the house, he would have added the porch. It stretched across the front and wrapped around both sides so that a breeze could be felt from all directions. He remembered that as a boy, there was always a shady area to play or a protected place away from the rain or wind. After adding the porch, he would draw the railings and the spindles. When he was young, there had seemed to be so many spindles and he remembered the stories of great-grandfather Archie, painstakingly turning each one by hand with a lathe.

He could picture the very spot where he and Brandon had slept in their sleeping bags on many a star-filled night. They would laugh at silly jokes, tell stories about their friends at school, and share secrets about their girlfriends. One time in the sixth grade, they had a crush on the same girl and there had been some tense moments between them. They had actually been mad at each other for two weeks, hollering, "Stupid," "No you're stupid!" and "Shut-up, you dumb head!" at each other. As it turned out, the girl didn't like either one of them and they had both felt pretty bummed out about it. At the next sleep over, they vowed to each other, "I promise to not ever like the same girl that you like" and "I sure miss you when we are mad at each other."

The foundation of the house was a pier and beam; up off the ground so that there was a crawl space under the porch. There was also a trap door by the front steps that led down into a cellar. One time when they were arguing about a report that they were working on together, Mike had gone into the house mad and Brandon had hidden under there for several hours. Mike had given up looking for him and had gone on into dinner. When Brandon's mom called the house looking for him, Mike had gone outside to look for him one more time. As he walked down the steps, Brandon had raised the trap door and sneaked up behind him. Mike had been scared out of his wits and had wrestled Brandon to the ground. They had a fistfight to beat all. "I hate you!" Mike had hollered.

Brandon hollered right back, "I hate you more!" They rolled around on the ground until Matt; Mike's dad had come out to tear them apart. He sure had good memories of how much fun he had hanging out with Brandon. He missed the carefree days of being a young boy.

This evening, as he slowly rocked in the porch swing, his eyes moved back and forth as he looked at the slats on the porch. They were double thickness, but when he would sketch them, he would sketch them running horizontally. They had been replaced several years ago in the same fashion that they had been originally installed. Once a year they needed a fresh coat of paint, because they would get worn and weathered looking. Then he noticed the plaque by the front door. He knew that Jake, his older brother, had worked really hard doing the research and filing the paperwork with The State Historic Preservation Office in order to get the house listed on the National Register. They had taken pictures of the ceremony when the plaque was presented and placed them in the Treasure Chests. There were also newspaper clippings and an article in a magazine that had been included.

    He knew that so many of his past relatives would be proud that the house had stood the test of time, was in such good shape, and was continually filled with love and laughter. Life had not been easy for any one of them. There had been some sad times, but the family had a closeness that helped them through it all. Some people would say that a porch was just a porch, but if this porch could talk, it would be able to tell of so many monumental occasions that occurred here. The porch could also recount all of the times that boys and girls alike would have pretended to play and daydream about their futures. It was almost eerie to Mike, how many of those imaginative futures had come to fruition. He had grown up hearing the stories of his distant and not so distant relatives and their childhood memories on this porch.

CHAPTER 5
THE HISTORY OF SPRINGFIELD

Springfield had been established in October of 1845 by a group of nine. They had decided to travel from the east, westward, on horseback to seek new opportunities and new homes. The leader of the group, John, had a father who had fought in the Revolutionary War. His father had been only eighteen when he fought in the war and then had moved his family numerous times around the country, always seeking adventure and a better way of life. John was eager to carry on his father's spirit of travel. The other frontiersmen that were with him included immigrants from Sweden, Germany, and Ireland. As they traveled, John would occasionally ask "What do you think about this section of land?"

One or the other would comment, "Let's keep on going, this land looks as if it might flood," or "There might be something better on up the way. Let's keep on riding."

They trekked many miles to find a suitable location for a new town. After several weeks, they agreed that it was getting too close to wintertime to spend much more time scouting any further west. That evening, they decided that it would be best if they built a makeshift sod hut for the winter and explore the surrounding land while they waited until spring.

One evening as they camped, John suggested, "Let's divide up into teams and spend our time building a soddie and then scout the land."

The Swede suggested that, "We can have three groups of three and work on gathering wood and sod for the hut, firewood for the winter, and stockpiling some wild game for food."

The "soddie," or sod house, faced the south for the warmth, and on the east side they built a lean-to for the horses and their gear. The soddie was built using wood and prairie sod patched with dirt in order to prevent leaks. They later bragged to those back home that the soddie had been quite warm in the winter and extremely cool in the summer. During that first long winter, when the weather cooperated, they would head out to explore the land that stretched as far as the eye could see. They quickly discovered that the land surrounding their cabin had some great qualities. Three of the nine came back one afternoon all excited about what they had seen.

The German commented, "There's plenty of flat, fertile land for crops. I can also picture beautiful ranches and farms on these rolling hills."

"The lumber is a little sparse," explained the Swede, "but we could use stones for wall boundaries and save the wood for the houses."

One of the other immigrants from Ireland, stated, "The springs just seem to bubble up out of the ground. There would be plenty of water for livestock."

They also discovered the land to have an abundance of wild game including prairie chickens, wild pigeons, wild turkeys, quail, deer, rabbits, and squirrels. The rivers and lakes were full of fish. They had plenty to eat that first winter.

They scouted the land each day and one evening when they were sharing stories of their discoveries, decided that this was about the most ideal place for them to settle and bring their families to. The leader asked them, "Let's take a vote and decide on whether this is a good place to put down our roots. Think about whether or not you want to bring your wives and children back here to live. We need to make a unified choice."

The men talked back and forth for hours, late into the night. One of the men said, "We like this land and we haven't felt afraid. The officials told us before we came this direction that the Native Americans had been removed to land farther west of here, so our settlement should be safe."

The Swede spoke up and stated, "I can picture my wife and my two little girls loving this land. Our native country was very much like this. The winters are just as cold as what we would be leaving behind, but springtime and its beauty would more than make up for that."

The immigrant from Germany commented, "This is good land and I miss my home country, but this reminds me so much of West Muensterland, the valley that I grew up in."

The Irish immigrant spoke up as well and said, " My wife sent me to find a safe piece of land that we can farm and raise crops. Everything about this part of the country will make her happy."

The leader proceeded by saying, "Let's take a vote!" One by one the men said, "Yes," "Ja," "Count me in," and "I'm with you on this."

The leader cast his vote with a certain "Yes!" and the decision was made. There was much celebrating that evening. Names for the town were discussed and they finally agreed that Springfield would be the perfect name for their town. The springs in the middle of the huge field.

Seven of the nine had families that they would be returning east to bring back in the spring. They wanted to make sure that this location would be safe and they had had an opportunity to build shelters for them. There was enough lumber and this place was near the crossing of a river that would supply plenty of water for drinking, a place to build a grain mill and future transportation. There were also two major trails that intersected close by, so the men agreed that there would be plenty of trade and commerce. Hopefully, in the near future, trains would be coming through this part of the country as well.

As time permitted, they built a few more structures, knowing that many of the families would be able to live out of their wagons for a while. The seven men that had families had returned to gather up their loved ones and their belongings. Returning as soon as possible, they built cabins large enough for each family. Word spread quickly that a new town was being established. Many came by the wagonload and Springfield had grown rapidly to include three churches, a school, a mill, a blacksmith, various stores, two banks, a hotel, homes, and cattle ranches.

The townsfolk were eager to help newcomers get established and almost every weekend there was either a barnraising or a pounding party. A barnraising was when all of the able bodied men would bring their tools and help a neighbor to build a new barn or building. The women would cook and feed everyone while the children would run and play tag. A pounding party was similar to a welcoming party where everyone would bring necessary household items and food to help a new family get settled in. Many an event would finish up with some fiddling and dancing. There was such a sense of devotion and caring. The town had certainly prospered and flourished.

Trade routes did include Springfield in their stops and as a result, there were always new products offered in the General Store. With the invention of the telegraph in 1835 by Samuel Morse, people had been able to communicate long distances and, in 1848, Springfield was one of the first towns for miles around to offer this form of communication. Stagecoaches brought mail and parcels, and visitors sometimes enjoyed themselves so much that they stayed and sent back east for their belongings. Eventually, the railroad bought land and laid track through the town. The railroads brought more and more people westward and more people meant more commerce, so Springfield had grown by leaps and bounds.

The original cabin remained in the middle of town with the businesses and homes branching outward. They changed the construction so that it could be preserved. By removing the sod and using logs, they chinked the open spaces with a mixture of mud and grass. They replaced the sod roofs with shakes. All of the original nine men eventually had families and they were active in the community. The town had hired a sheriff and, as the community had grown, they had set up a government that included a mayor and other public officials.

After becoming a state in 1846, the state had favored the sentiments of the North, but fifteen years later, many of the families were divided as they sent sons off to fight against each other. The Civil War greatly affected the small town. The old-timers told stories for years about the afternoon that the telegraph operator had rushed over to the newspaper editor to tell him that Fort Sumter had been attacked. The mayor had called a town meeting to discuss the ramifications of war in their close-knit community. They met that very evening to vote and call up a regiment.

The group had met to have a discussion, but it was obvious that the opinions were divided. One gentleman began by suggesting, "If we are going to establish a regiment, we need to do everything we can to ensure our boys' safety. We need proper clothing, gear, and weapons. I sure don't want my son going off to war, but if he does, I want him to have what he needs."

Right away, one of the dissenters hollered from the back, "I think that we are crazy for even considering this. Why don't we just keep our noses out of this?"

Someone else countered, "The south is fighting for slavery, and we won't have it."

That's when the debate began. They tried to speak calmly about slavery and what the South was wanting. Others spoke about the North and the beliefs that all men should be free.

The atmosphere became more tense when one of the boys stood up and announced, "I am heading off to fight for the South. My cousins live down there and they are Americans too, and all they want is to be left alone! You all just seem to have your heads turned backwards."

Before he had a chance to sit down, his dad grabbed him by the sleeve and hollered, "Come on, son. We're out of here. Anyone else have relatives in the south or thinking that they have their rights just like we have ours? Let's go!"

Several others jumped up angrily, shoving their chairs around, just daring someone to say something. They left the group to do what they had come to do. The remaining supporters elected leaders for the regiment and put together resources so that they could equip and provide all that the men and boys would need. No one was happy to be sending loved ones off to war.

There had been talk about the young man and his family. Many couldn't believe that one of their own would fight for the Confederacy, but secretly wondered how all of this fighting would end up. The young man never came home again. His father learned later that he had died at the Battle of Vicksburg. Many of the other families lost loved ones as well. Fathers, sons, brothers, uncles, and many close friends were to never come home to Springfield except to be buried. The war had taken a deadly toll on their close knit community.

CHAPTER 6
THE FOURTH OF JULY 1895

"Springfield is celebrating 50 YEARS and Archie and Jewell are having an OPEN HOUSE"

The year was 1895 and the town was fifty years old. It was the Fourth of July and a wonderful time for a grand celebration. The entire town and the surrounding areas had come out to the Pioneer Park for a long weekend of food and festivities. The park had been designed with the original cabin in the middle. It was hard to imagine that nine men were able to withstand that first, harsh, snowy winter in that small, dank cabin. Trees had been planted to form a square around the perimeter of the park and benches and paths had been laid out so that all ages could gather and mingle throughout the year. You could always see older men whittling and trading stories about the olden days as well as boys running around, chasing each other, and looking for mischief.

The women had baked, cooked, sewn, and gathered memorabilia for days. The excitement had escalated as they had decorated their tables and laid out their fine tablecloths and quilts for the festivities. July 4 was on a Thursday and the town was able to celebrate beginning on Wednesday evening and continuing through the weekend. The children had been so excited that they were able to play games and party for five days. They had been busy with their friends and decorated their wagons, tricycles and bikes for the Grand Parade that was held on Thursday morning at ten o'clock. Prizes were awarded for the best decorated in each category, the most authentic patriotic costume, the most delectable baked goods, and the most original quilt. Some of the old-timers spoke about the way life was when the town was established and people that had moved away had returned for the huge reunion that was held in the new, brick school house that had recently been completed.

One of the most exciting events that the entire town had looked forward to was the unveiling of the Chautauqua. The Chautauqua was an octagon shaped structure that was to be used for entertainment and cultural events. It was part of a social movement that had spread from Chautauqua, New York across the United States. Many towns would set up tents for the traveling Chautauqua circuit. The circuit would include guest speakers, educational programs, cultural exhibits, and musical performances to name just a few. The country as a whole was becoming more interested in the arts and Springfield wanted to be ahead of the times. Springfield had been fortunate enough to build a permanent structure of wood. The entire community had voted unanimously to spend the necessary money. They knew that they would have so many uses for the building.

The children had been sneaking peeks through the temporary fence that had been constructed around it until it was ready for the public to see. They would run home and report to their friends and families what had been done recently. One little boy had raced around the town on his bicycle hollering, "They put the cupola on top of the auditorium today. I counted twenty-four windows and it's ripping!"

The mayor even had a costume sewn to look like President Grover Cleveland. They had invited the president to attend, but he had declined, so the mayor had dressed up. He had come out on the stage with baskets full of surprises. He mimicked President Cleveland and bellowed in his huge, throaty voice, "Do you know what I have in these baskets? Goetze's Bubble Gum and Woodward's Real Butter Scotch Candy. There will be a bubble blowing contest after lunch by the Chautauqua." He threw handfuls of them out into the crowd, almost creating a riot as everyone scrambled for a treat.

Booths and displays had been set up all around the park. The one that caught the attention of the children, along with their parents, was the display sponsored by the Kellogg's company. A new cereal named Granose had been developed. Dr. John Harvey Kellogg, the superintendent of Michigan's Battle Creek Sanitarium, needed a healthy alternative for the typical breakfast foods of that time. Many of his patients were vegetarians and did not eat meat. The advertisements showed Granose to be a healthy substitute for animal foods such as bacon and sausage. The patent was pending, but there were samples for sale. The ten-ounce packages had sold for fifteen cents and were gone after the first two days. In later years, the product name was changed to Corn Flakes.

The entertainment started each day at sunup and went long past dark. Thursday, Friday, and Saturday nights had live music and dancing. After the ribbon cutting of the Chautauqua, the townspeople used it for many of the activities. Later in history, Theodore Roosevelt had been quoted as saying that Chautauqua was "the most American thing in America!" The town's people could not have agreed more. They were so proud of what Springfield had become in the past fifty years and hoped for an equally prosperous future.

Some of the young men had been assembling torches to use for extra light, after the sun went down each evening. The torches along with the gas lanterns that lined the square painted a beautiful picture in the moonlight. Anyone that wanted to participate had been encouraged to be a part of the festivities. It was a party to beat all parties.

The mission-styled house with the porch was having a party on this celebration weekend as well. It was finally finished and it seemed like a fitting time to have an afternoon Open House. They chose Sunday after church, a time when the activities were winding down at the square. It was, by far, the largest house in the town and sat on an acre of slightly sloped land. There were three huge oak trees in the front yard and five dogwood trees and two birch trees in the back and side yards. The house was built on the land so that it would be shaded by these stately trees. The builders of the house had been bringing in supplies and furnishings by wagons, riverboats, and trains for the past nine months and they were finally ready to invite everyone to celebrate with them. They had placed a full-page invitation in the paper. It read:

You are cordially invited
To an
OPEN HOUSE
At the home of Jewell and Archibald
Sunday, July 7th, 2-5 p.m.
115 Oak Hill Lane

Some of Archibald's friends in college had been studying to be architects and builders. They studied and learned from famous designers such as Frank Lloyd Wright, George Washington Maher, and many others. These architects were combining architectural styles from Europe and re-designing the trends for new projects in the United States. The students were eager to graduate and get started on their own careers.

Archie and Jewell had asked one of these architect friends to help with their house. Their friend had used the couple's ideas, sketched some drawings, and then drawn up the floor plans for the contractor to use throughout construction. The style of the house was referred to as an Arts and Crafts house, a Prairie School style, or a Mission style house. They had combined brick, stone, stucco, and shingles with the usual building materials.

After enlisting the help from some local builders and craftsmen, the house that had once been a dream had become a reality. Obviously, the town had been very curious about this wonderful new home that had been built.

Archie was known as a character that loved the newest inventions. The house was said to have many of the latest products that the townsfolk had only read about or seen in *The Springfield Daily* or *The Farmer's Almanac*. Jewell was proud to demonstrate her new electric iron, fan and mixer in the kitchen. Archie had established the first furniture store on the square when he moved to town in the late 1880's. People had always come from miles around to place their orders for furniture as well as stoves, clocks, radios, and furnishings. Archie was frequently off to the East Coast to shop for new and different styles of furnishings that he brought back and offered to his customers. Friends stopped by the store, just to talk and learn about all of the new inventions that Archie had seen on his travels.

When he and Jewell married in 1890, they were both almost twenty-five and had been ready to settle down and raise a family. They lived in a small home to the east of the square while they saved, designed, and built their new home. It took a long time, in those days, to build a house. Supplies did not always arrive on time and so much of the house was built by hand.

Archie and Jewell were so thrilled that the construction was complete. As they stood on the porch and admired the finished product, Archie hugged Jewell and whispered to her, "I am so proud of what we have been able to accomplish. I can't wait to have people over. Now, we will have room for our friends and families to come and visit."

Jewell agreed, "We are truly blessed! The house, the Fourth of July and the fifty-year celebration of Springfield will all be at the same time! We are going to have so much fun this weekend and hopefully for a long, long time to come!"

The front door of the house entered into a large foyer with a hall that stretched through the center of the house. It was referred to as a living hall because all of the rooms anchored off of this walkway. The staircase was at the front of the house leading up to two large bedrooms and an open sitting area. Downstairs, the living areas were large, basically square rooms to be used as the dining room, the living room, the master bedroom, and the kitchen area. Off of the back of the kitchen, there were steps going into the back yard and then outside steps into the basement.

The exterior walls of the house had floor to ceiling cedar shingle, sidewall shakes painted a pale yellow. The trim was a crisp white and the porch was painted a light gray. The roof was covered with dark colored wood shingles. There were wide concrete stairs leading up to the porch. The numbers for the address were to the left of the front door even though everyone in town knew this house. There were two large windows on the front of the house-one on each side of the front door. On the second level, there was a double dormer in the center of the roofline that featured two windows, one for each of the upstairs bedrooms.

Archie and Jewell included new ideas in this house in order to make it unique. The concept of closets had been new and this house had one in each room. There was even something called a butler's pantry in the kitchen that would have been used for extra food and dishes. There was an indoor toilet both on the first floor and one on the second. The kitchen had a large fireplace as well as a stove. The citizens of Springfield could not wait to take a tour of this fabulous home.

The Fourth of July had been a huge success for the town of Springfield and for Archie and Jewell. All afternoon, at the open-house, there had been a steady stream of well-wishers. That evening as they cleaned up, Archie had commented to Jewell, "This has been one of the happiest days of my life. Next to the day I married you, my beautiful bride, this day has made me very thankful for my life."

The Porch

Jewell hugged him tightly and agreed, "I'm very happy also and maybe now that we have this huge project behind us, we can focus on starting our family. I dream of this house, this porch, and this yard to be full of laughter and children playing." They had laughed together and finished the rest of the dishes. Jewell spent the following days, handwriting thank-you notes. Many of their visitors had brought gifts for the new home; the town's generosity had been overwhelming.

The porch was designed for entertaining, and entertaining they did. Jewell hosted tea parties, Archie had friends over to play dominoes, and together they served dinner to many of the families of Springfield. They spoke often of rocking children and grandchildren on the porch, under the shade of the majestic oak trees, yet it was five long years before they were blessed with a child. Archie fondly remembered the candlelight dinner when one evening, Jewell had him open a small gift that she had placed by his plate. He took his time, mentally trying to think about anniversary and birthday dates. Had he missed something that she had remembered? Inside had been a small bib that said, "I Love My Daddy." Archie had jumped up and run to Jewell's side and lifted her up into his arms like a small child. He twirled her around and around until they were almost dizzy. As he set her down, there were tears in his eyes. He gulped back his emotions and told her how much he loved her. They were finally going to have a baby!

Sara was a beautiful, dainty child with slight features. Her hair was short, reddish blond, her eyes were deep blue, and she had the sweetest lips. She was a quiet baby and loved to be rocked, but she also loved to play and entertained herself easily. Archie thought that she was the most beautiful little girl that he had ever seen. Jewell envisioned dressing Sara in frilly dresses and teaching her all of the manners of their time. As most parents, dreams about their children's futures are usually dreams that they had for themselves.

CHAPTER 7
TEN YEAR OLD SARA-1910

At the age of ten, Sara was anything but plain and simple looking. She had a natural beauty about her, with freckles on her nose and upper cheekbones. The dimples on her cheeks sunk inward like small craters when she smiled broadly. When the other girls talked about curling their hair and wearing makeup, Sara was not in the least bit interested. She was polite as she listened to them discuss the new Max Factor studio in Los Angeles and what all of the actresses were doing in order to look more glamorous.

Sara was a unique young lady and when you passed her on the street you might smile and think to yourself that she was not aware of how beautiful she would be when she was a little older, wearing some powder, and a little bit of rouge. Her hair was shoulder length, reddish blond, and there were always wisps of it that fell out of place and onto her forehead. She had the most natural way of using her hand to flip them behind her ears, yet they spilled right back out again.

Her eyes always seemed to be looking off into the distance or maybe the future. Her parents, Archie and Jewell were constantly playing twenty questions with her, trying to figure out where her mind was wandering off to. Sara's hair had natural curl, but she brushed it nightly, secretly wishing that it were straight as a board. She wore it full around her shoulders, to please her mother. If she had it her way, it would be pulled back into a ponytail or a braid. Her nose was small and her lips were parted as if she was about to speak. Her eyes were a deep blue and full of mystery and surprise. She was a child that looked as if she knew a secret that no one else knew. Her mother, Jewell, dressed her far too fussy for playing on the porch, yet Sara did not really own any play clothes. She often thought to herself, *Someday I will be old enough to make up my own mind about how I want to dress. It might not be my mother's style, but I will be happy.* She knew that she would not be wearing frilly dresses all of the time. A nurse would wear a crisp, starched uniform and working long hours would not afford the time for so much primping and fussing.

Sara was setting up her play area on the porch. It had been rainy and windy all week and she was using an old trunk that her dad had brought home from work. When she opened it up on its end, she could set up her hospital inside and her stuff would stay dry and not blow away. Her patients were all types, shapes, and sizes. They were paper dolls, cloth dolls, and dolls that had porcelain heads, arms, and legs. Her imagination and pretend play was well beyond her years. She had overheard the grownups talking about the soldiers that had been so brutally injured during the battles of the Spanish-American War and her heart ached to think of the pain that they had felt during the healing of their injuries. Archie read to her daily from the newspaper and she learned about political events and foreign affairs. When she was little, he had read her as many books as he could find about doctors and nurses. As she learned to read on her own, she always had a library book about nursing. Some of them she had read over and over again. One of her favorites had been about Doctor Walter Reed and all of his efforts to stop the spread of yellow fever and malaria, diseases that had killed so many. Sara had also imagined how lonely the workers at the Panama Canal would have been as they lay in the hospital beds wondering if they would ever see their families again. Many of them were young and they would have been missing their parents and their homes.

These were some of the ideas that Sara used as she pretended to practice nursing. She would spend hours on the porch making up stories about situations that the wounded or ill were experiencing. The patients were lined up, row after row, some with head bandages and some with arm or leg bandages. Many needed wet rags on their heads for the fever and small bottles filled with colored water were used for medicines. She wiped their brows and comforted them with soothing words. "You're so brave. I know that it hurts so badly, but I think that with a little time, you will be better and will be able to go home. I know that your family must be worried about you." The next one might hear, "Just a little bit of this medicine. Your fever is about to break. Maybe in the morning you will be able to try a little broth." She knew in her heart that she would be a good nurse. She felt patient and kind and used a soothing voice when she quietly tended to her soldiers and her patients.

As Sara sat on the porch, gazing off into space, she daydreamed about all sorts of adventures that she hoped would happen in her future. As she held her doll close she mused, "Will I travel and be a nurse in a foreign country or go to a nursing school and teach others about disease, treatments, and compassion? Will I teach small children at orphanages about hygiene or will I work for a doctor and do all of the tasks that will help him during surgery?"

On this particular afternoon, a passerby would think that Sara was pretending to be at a party or somewhere very social. Sara and her favorite doll were dressed in matching outfits, dresses that looked as if they were off to an afternoon tea. Sara was nothing like the image that a stranger might assume. Her mother had been entertaining her bridge group and she had dressed Sara in her Sunday clothing. The doll had matching clothes because that was one of the gifts that her mother had given her for her tenth birthday. She couldn't wait for everyone to leave so that she could go back to her make believe play.

Jewell didn't want to accept the fact that Sara was not like the other ladies' daughters. She was so focused on pretending to be a nurse and would spend all of her free time playing on the porch. For her birthday, Sara had asked for unusual types of gifts. She wanted a journal, a fountain pen, a medical kit with realistic items (like a syringe and a stethoscope), books about medical conditions, and a sewing kit to practice sewing up wounds. Sara had received all that she asked for, but as she had opened them, her mother had acted as if the gifts were frivolous and silly.

Her mother had saved the "best" present for last. Sara had tried to act excited about the gift as she tore into the box. There were mounds of tissue and underneath, there it was! One of the largest teddy bears that money could buy. President Theodore Roosevelt had been on a hunting expedition several years before and the only animal that he had come across was a small bear cub. He could not bring himself to shoot it and days later the story appeared in the newspapers. A cartoonist had illustrated the incident in the *Washington Post*. Two days later a toy maker had the cartoon displayed next to a stuffed brown bear in his storefront window. The "teddy bear" had caught on and Jewell had wanted her daughter to be one of the first in town to have one. Sara hugged each of her parents tightly. She knew that they both loved her very much and her birthday had been wonderful.

Her father Archie understood her personality better than anyone else. He was a progressive-type man, wanting to learn all that he could about everything. He had been a furniture salesman as far back as Sara could remember, but recently had sold the business and had opened a Ford dealership. He would come home from work, so excited about the people that he met and the stories that he heard. Sara would hang on his every word as he recanted tales that customers had shared with him from their travels both near and far. She thought to herself, *Someday, I'll leave this town and I will travel. I will have adventures that no one here would even imagine in their wildest dreams. I shall return home and tell of my marvelous times to my loved ones!*

The day after her birthday, her daddy had come from work to find her once again, playing nurse on the porch. He teasingly asked her, "Sara, Have you given your new bear a name?"

Sara answered carefully, out of respect for her mother, "I think that the best name would be Teddy. Mother is so excited that I have him out here with me while her friends come over for tea."

Archie, tried to tease her a bit more about the bear, "Will you be making him a hospital gown to wear so that he matches your other patients?"

"Oh, daddy," she sighed, "you know that bears don't need treatments like these patients do. My soldiers that have fever need alcohol baths and the ones with cholera need bed-rest. Mother would die if I started stitching wounds and putting lavoris on Teddy."

Daddy tried once more to get a giggle out of Sara. He worried that she was much too serious for a ten-year-old. "Has my little girl gotten too old to play dolls with a stuffed animal?

The Porch

At that, Sara laughed out loud and smiled one of her beautiful smiles that always seemed to melt her daddy's heart.

Sara's house was about fifteen years old, but it felt like a new house to her. Archie had spent many a long hour, working on keeping the house in perfect shape. He was always painting or repairing something and, lately, his hobby was to add every new invention that he could order from the mail-order catalogs. Each pay check was brought home and Sara's mother and father would sit at the kitchen table pouring over the bills and budgeting for the things that they had to spend money on and the gadgets that her father wanted to buy next. Jewell complained that they were spending too much money on "toys," yet as she entertained her bridge ladies she showed off their latest purchases.

Archie had been listening to the news, learning all that he could about electricity. The house had been built with basic electricity, but there were so many new gadgets that they could own if their wiring was upgraded. They had recently updated their indoor plumbing and they were one of the first families to have a telephone. Sara smiled to herself and thought, *A telephone is fine if you have someone to call. Maybe one of these days, we can use ours when our friends and neighbors get one.*

Sara was playing alone on the porch, not because she didn't have any friends, but because none of them wanted to play the same way that she wanted to play. She longed for a good friend to play nurse with, but the other girls always wanted to play dress up and tea party with their dolls. She sometimes felt that she was more like the boys in the neighborhood. The adventure of running around outside, hiding, and pretending to shoot at each other looked like a lot more fun. She wished that they would let her be the nurse for their pretend injuries from their pretend battles, but when she suggested that idea they would run off hollering, "No girls allowed!"

Feeling different about life, must have been a trait that she had inherited from her father. He said that he loved this old house because it was different from all of the other houses on the block. When Archie had owned the furniture store, he had been able to get all of the proper furnishings for the Arts and Crafts style of the house, and, at Christmas time, they would have an open house for all of the neighbors, their friends, and all of their friends' children.

Sara had to admit that it was a beautiful home, no matter what the occasion, and her parents were very open and warm people. She especially loved this porch. It always had a shady spot to play and the way that it wrapped around the corners of the house, there was room to set up her hospital with plenty of beds to care for her patients. She would write in her journal, keeping track of all of her patients and what they had wrong with them and how she had helped them. She would also record some of the interesting stories that her father told from work. She had read and learned about famous nurses. The one that she had learned the most from was Florence Nightingale, the "Lady with the Lamp." Florence Nightingale had proved that good nursing and a clean hospital helped to prevent infection and death. Reading about Nurse Nightingale had convinced Sara even more that she could make a difference in her world by becoming a nurse.

CHAPTER 8
"THE TREASURE CHEST"

It was the summer after Sara's tenth birthday and the town readied itself for the annual Fourth of July celebration. It was also family reunion time and as every year before, and hopefully every year from then on, the entire clan had assembled to catch up on all of the news and see all of the new babies that had been added to the family. Archie had come from a large family and many of his brothers and sisters visited for the long weekend. July 4, 1910, was on a Monday and there was an extra day to travel and enjoy each other's company. Jewell had one sister, but she and her husband had been blessed with four children, two girls and two boys. They did not visit often, but when they did, it was tons of fun. The house was all-abuzz and the porch was decorated with the traditional patriotic bunting. It stretched across the front of the eaves and around the sides and made one want to stop and salute the flag right then and there.

Sara had to put all of her dolls and such away in order to make room for the extra seating that would be on the porch. Even though she would not be pretending to play nurse for a few days, she was excited about the upcoming events. There would be a carnival atmosphere at the Pioneer Park with all types of candies, kettle popcorn, and good foods to sample. There would also be a baked goods contest and her mother had been planning for weeks. She and Sara had gone through all of the recipes and decided which ones they would bake for the long weekend. As she helped to decorate, she asked her mother Jewell, "How many people will be staying at our house this year? How many people will be staying at the neighbor's houses? Can all of the girl cousins stay in my room? We can sleep on the floor and have such a good time staying up late and telling stories to each other. They are more fun than any of the girls that I know around here."

Jewell laughed at her daughter's excitement and answered her, "You asked me so many questions that I don't know which one to answer first. I think that we will have fifteen extra people, five will be staying at the Wilson's house, and three will be staying at the Morris's house and, yes, the girls can all stay in your room. I'm glad that you look forward to this time of the year so much."

When Archie built the house back in 1895, he was so into clever add-ons. He had read about the large mansions and how they had special cellars to keep ice in so that they could serve cold beverages throughout the warm months. He had decided to build such a cellar under the front porch. It had been dug out and constructed with stone before the house was even started. Once the porch was in place, a trap door had been concealed under the porch slats. If one knew where it was, one could open the door in the slats, unlock the trap door, and retrieve the ice that was stored down below. It worked so well that it could be filled up with blocks of ice in the winter and then chiseled off of until the next winter when it was refilled. The neighbors and townsfolk loved to be invited over to sit on the porch with a tall glass of iced tea or cold lemonade.

Now that the family had an icebox in the house, he bought ice for it and kept drinks cool inside. Archie had decided to clean out the cellar under the front porch. He spent several weekends airing it out and repairing the steep steps that went down into the eight-foot square opening. He had grand plans of using the space to store keepsakes and memorabilia. He bought an old nail and hardware box from the hardware store and weatherproofed it with paint and waxed paper. Archie and Jewell spent hours going through the family records and information, pictures and keepsakes. His goal was to create a time capsule so in years to come future relatives would have plenty of information about the history of the house and the family.

One evening, when the project was almost complete, he spent some time showing the items to Sara and explaining his thoughts for the crates. "Sara, I know that right now you are young and a lot of these items that your mother and I are putting in here look like junk to you and have very little meaning. I hope that as the years go by, you will listen to the stories about this memorabilia and will eventually add your own things to the "Treasure Chest." When you are a grown woman and your mother and I have passed away or are too old to remember details, you will be the one to pass on the histories and the tradition."

From the serious tone of Archie's voice, Sara understood how important this was to her father and answered with a polite, "Yes, sir." Her mind had already been wondering what types of memories and treasures that she would have from her career of nursing and her travels to faraway places that she would be able to add to the crate.

July 4, 1910, commemorated the family Treasure Chest and items that the family members brought to the reunion were discussed, recorded in a journal, and placed into the crate for safekeeping until the next year. In the journal, they recorded who was able to attend and kept an account of births and deaths in the family. The family all agreed that it was a great idea and wondered how large this family would grow and would they ever run out of room under the porch.

When Archie and Jewell had gathered up all of the items that had been passed down from their parents, they had found immigration records from passenger arrival records, ship manifests, and family Bibles that had birth and death information. They also found coins and stamps along with several old pictures and postcards. They included these items after displaying them on tables at the Fourth of July reunion. Archie and Jewell had also agreed that the Treasure Chest would be a very safe place to put the original plans of the house and an inventory of everything that they had purchased when it was being built.

Archie had gone through all of the special items that he had accrued before he had sold the furniture store. He had some special papers, awards, and a special Japanese puzzle box. He cataloged all of them in to the journal and placed them into the Treasure Chest. He had bought the puzzle box as a souvenir on his last shopping trip to the East Coast. It was a small box with a secret compartment and he wondered at the time, if anyone would be able to figure out how it worked. Archie opened and shut the box numerous times, until he felt confident that he understood the directions that had come with it. In the secret compartment, he had placed a strip of paper with five numbers printed on it. He secretly mused, *I don't know when this box will be opened and when these numbers will be discovered. I hope that when the time is right, these numbers will be a clue for that person to use. He or she will hopefully use the numbers to solve a mystery that will lead him or her to important papers.* He intentionally did *not* put the directions for the box and what the numbers were for when he wrote in the journal.

The most special of all of Archie's additions for this year was the new picture that had just been taken of Henry Ford and himself cutting the ribbon at the new Ford dealership. There had also been pictures of everyone in the family taking turns driving around town in the new Model T that Archie had brought home for the occasion.

The Porch

After many years in the furniture business, Archie had heard about a new opportunity. In 1896, Henry Ford had developed a car called the Quadricycle. It was basically a small two-cylinder gasoline engine on a frame with four bicycle wheels. Twelve years later, Ford developed the Model T. He called it the "universal car" and Americans fondly referred to it as the "Tin Lizzie." Fifteen million of this automobile alone were sold until 1927. The price for each automobile started out high, $825, but assembly-line manufacturing eventually helped to lower the price to less than $300. Archie had just begun a new chapter in his life. Archie did not know it yet, but his new Ford dealership was in store for much prosperity and growth.

Henry Ford was marketing his new automobiles and was looking for aspiring gentlemen willing to take a risk, never before imagined. After much conversation around the kitchen table, he and Jewell had decided that it was worth the risk and the challenge. They had made a wise decision about how to invest their money. They opened a Ford dealership; the only one for miles around. If the popularity of owning a car caught on, they would do quite well. If not, then Archie and Jewell would be broke.

Archie went through training as he learned all about automobiles, but he was already known as a fair and respected salesman. The major consideration about this investment was the sizable amount of money that he and Jewell had to use from their savings. As Sara dozed off to sleep many nights, she listened to them discuss their plans for the future. She worried silently to herself, *If this deal that mom and dad are thinking about, doesn't work out, will we lose our house with our beautiful porch?*

CHAPTER 9
SARA IS A NURSE

In the fall of 1917, Sara was a first year nursing student. She had studied diligently in high school and had graduated with honors. Many of her friends were hoping to get married and start their families, but Sara was focused on her future. Throughout the years, she had never changed her mind about nursing; in fact she loved it more than she could have ever imagined.

So many doctors and nurses had gone off to the war in Europe that there was a shortage of them at home. The nursing school had worked out a plan to incorporate class time with volunteer time for the students. She had been able to work as many hours as her body would allow her to and she arrived home so exhausted, barely able to eat a bite before she fell asleep. Sara would wake early to do her homework so that she could make top grades in her classes. She seemed to have a good mind for all of the tedious memorizing and reading that was required.

In 1916, Woodrow Wilson had won his second term as President and it appeared that the efforts of the United States to stay neutral were waning. The United States had yet to enter the Great War. His second term campaign slogan had been "He kept us out of war." It was a close election and the country held its breath for three days to find out who had won. They waited on the electoral votes from California. His opponent, Charles Evans Hughes, had gone to bed the night before the announcement, thinking that he had won the election. Someone in his household answered the phone the next morning. A reporter asked to speak to Mr. Hughes. He was told that the president was sleeping. The reporter replied, "Tell him that he is not the president," and hung up.

As time progressed, the country was slowly dragged into the problems across the Atlantic. In January of 1917, Germany had announced that it would resume unrestricted submarine activity in British waters. On April 2, President Wilson asked Congress to declare war against Germany. War was declared on April 6 and the United States joined the Allied Powers. By the spring of 1918, there were more than a million Americans stationed in France and Belgium.

Woodrow Wilson gave a speech in January of 1918. He and his team of 150 advisors had formulated a peace program. His Fourteen Point Statement outlined a policy of free trade, open agreements, democracy, and self-determination. It was not until November 11, 1918, that an Armistice was reached; the "eleventh hour of the eleventh day of the eleventh month" of 1918. As a result of his peace efforts, Woodrow Wilson received the Nobel Peace Prize in 1919, for his determination and leadership.

While all of the unrest was occurring around the world, there was something equally critical going on closer to home. It was the spring of 1918 and Sara had had mixed emotions about her newest opportunity. The American Red Cross had been established in 1881 by Clara Barton along with a circle of friends. Their initial purpose was to aid the injured war soldiers during the Civil War. The organization had been active ever since and was now in need of more volunteer workers for the flu epidemic. Each volunteer would be given a day off from their jobs in exchange for their help in the hospitals. Sara was ready to offer her nursing skills for her fellow mankind. The Spanish Flu or "La Grippe" was raging throughout the country. No one knew for sure where the virus had originated but it was transmitted throughout the United States by sailors arriving in the port of Boston. It quickly spread to men mobilizing and training in military camps across the nation. The next fall, the flu was even worse. Every day Sara heard horrible stories about entire families being wiped out by the sickness and many small children being orphaned and sent to live with relatives elsewhere. During October alone, the death toll was 200,000. When the war ended and Americans celebrated with Armistice Day parades and large parties, the flu spread and casualties grew even greater. In November and December of that year, more people died than were born.

Because of the shortage of doctors and nurses in the United States, Sara's profession was in high demand. Besides being a volunteer at the local hospital, she traveled to neighboring hospitals. Each morning when she woke up she had been thankful that she was not sick. Doctors and nurses all around her were contracting the flu and many had even died.

All of her reading and studying had not prepared her for this chapter in her life. She continued to attend class, the ones that had not been cancelled, and in the late hours of the night would work on her projects and assignments. One evening when she and Archie were visiting before bedtime, her father had asked, "Sara, have you considered being more than a nurse and going to school for a longer time to become a doctor? Our country sure seems to need more doctors."

She thought about his suggestion for a while and as she replied, she realized that the answer was a simple one for her. "That might be something that someone else would want to do, but I want to be able to spend more time with my patients and be able to sit by their beds and minister to them in a tender and caring way."

It was ironic in a way. She had such a hard time having friends growing up, many felt that she had too quiet of a personality, yet when she could minister to a patient's needs her personality would come shining through. She was able to talk to her patients and, even more importantly, she took the time to be a good listener. As she tended to a young boy who had such a high fever and was not expected to live, she had overheard some of the other nurses talking about the latest Red Cross Bulletin. The numbers were out and it had been determined that more people were dying from the flu than from the war. The troops had brought it home with them and there had actually been boatloads full of sick and dying soldiers. What had started out as her adventure had become a career dealing with a very serious situation. She had known that at any time she herself might become ill and possibly die. The mood at the hospitals had become very solemn and each day she had to deal with so much sickness and death.

One day as she ate her lunch with some of her friends, she felt that someone was watching her. Before she turned around, she asked her friends, "Is there someone behind me, staring at me?"

They giggled and answered, "That's the new intern that we think is just so cute! He's a catch and you are such a lucky lady that he is watching you!"

She turned nonchalantly, but as their eyes met, his face broke into a cute, boyish grin. She shyly smiled back, and turned back to her lunch. She did not think much about the encounter until a week later when she and a few friends were again eating lunch. A group of about four or five interns came laughing and strolling through the cafeteria. The other girls already knew the interns' names and Sara found out that the one she had seen staring at her was named Robert. He was as outgoing as she was shy and it didn't take him long to find excuses to catch up with her in a hall or walk her home from work.

Because of their long workdays and busy class schedules, Sara and Robert spent most of their free time on the porch. Sara had continued to live at home with her parents and now Robert was becoming a permanent fixture as well. Robert was such a good fit for their family. He was always telling a story that Archie loved to hear and Sara's mother could tell her bridge friends that her daughter was falling in love with a doctor. Part of Sara's dreams of becoming a nurse had included going to some exciting parts of the world and helping people that needed help so desperately. She hesitated to let herself fall in love, because it might mean a change in her future plans. Sara could also not imagine life without Robert and she had learned about compromise from her parents. Robert wanted to do great things as a doctor and he promised that as soon as he finished medical school, they would travel and fulfill their dreams together.

Sara knew that she loved Robert and wanted to spend her life with him. In the spring of 1920, when all of the trees were blooming and the garden was full of fragrant flowers, they had been married on the steps of the porch. It was a beautiful, outdoor wedding and most of the town attended. Her mother and father hosted one of the most elegant parties that had ever been held at that comfortable home. Robert moved into the house with Sara and her parents. Money was tight and it just seemed like the right thing to do. Sara had never imagined living anywhere else, even though she had so many places that she wanted to travel and see.

CHAPTER 10
SARA AND ROBERT

It was July 4, 1920, and Family Reunion time again. The relatives had all gathered for a delicious picnic spread and sharing of news and memories. The latest fad was the I-Scream-Bars that Archie and Jewell had bought for the occasion. A young man named Christian Kent Nelson, age twenty-seven, owned a confectionery store. A customer could not decide if he should choose ice cream or a chocolate bar. "Why not put the chocolate around the ice cream and hold it with a stick?" he later asked himself. For the next four weeks he experimented with recipes for the chocolate covering. When he finally found a mixture that would stay on the ice cream, he made 500 of them and sold them at a local charity function. Archie was one of his best customers that year!

  They once again lifted the wooden crates from below the porch and assembled the memorabilia on folding tables. Sara had decided to add her handkerchief and a program from her wedding day to the keepsakes. There were also some pictures in an envelope with notes about those that had been able to attend

As the relatives had examined the memorabilia, several had studied the Japanese puzzle box and wondered what the significance of it was, but no one really discussed it and why it was there. Archie had watched each year as the box was studied and wondered when someone would specifically ask about it and why he had placed it in the Treasure Chest. As was tradition, all of the keepsakes were carefully wrapped and stored in the crates to be opened again the next year.

After several years, Robert and Sara had been able to move into a place of their own. The town was small and they did not live far from Sara's parents and the house with the porch. She and Robert had continued to work at the same hospital where they had met and most of the time had the same schedule. Family get-togethers were usually at her parents' house and it was at one of these special family times that Sara announced that she and Robert were expecting their first baby. Everyone was so excited.

As months went by, Sara's nursing job became more tiring and difficult as she got closer to the birth of the baby. Robert was still in medical school and they spent countless hours trying to figure out names for the baby and how they could afford all of the things that a new baby would need. The best solution that they were able to come up with was to move back in with Sara's parents. Of course, Jewell and Archie were thrilled. They had always wanted a house full of children and they had been disappointed when it seemed that Sara would be their only child. Jewell had to fight the urge to take over getting everything ready for the baby.

When Matt was born in 1922, they all thought that he was the most perfect little baby boy. He was born with a full head of dark brown hair and long beautiful eyelashes. One of the neighbors had commented when she brought food over to the family, "He should have come with his own razor." They had laughed and wondered how old he would be when he would need his first haircut. His complexion was a little darker than the relatives on Sara's side of the family. Robert's family had dark features and Sara wondered if he would grow up having dark hair with a reddish tint.

Sara was very happy with her role as a wife and a mother, but as she had rocked Matt on the front porch, she could not help but remember all of the dreams she had had as a child. She thought that her life would have had more adventure by now and there were times that she felt as if she was missing out on something. These thoughts would quickly pass, as her life was busy and full. Life was full of twists and turns and unexpected diversions.

Soon after Matt was born, Sara gave birth to a beautiful daughter that she and Robert named Mary. The year was 1924 and the house was crowded, so once again they made plans to move back to a place of their own. As soon as Robert finished his residency, he would be ready to set up his practice. She and Robert would often share their dreams of adventure with each other. He had learned so much about the world as he had treated the patients that had been off to the war and, he could not wait to travel and practice medicine. Sara agreed that as soon as the children were older, they would travel as a family and work as a team, she as a nurse and Robert as the doctor. Her dreams were soon to be dashed.

CHAPTER 11
EXCITEMENT AND DESPAIR

Much time had passed and the children were now off to school each day. Sara was able to practice nursing again fulltime and Robert was part of a group of general practitioners in Springfield. Sara's parents were still in the family home and they would all have such a good time together on the weekends. They visited on the porch and shared their lives with each other. On one particularly warm summer evening, Archie brought home a surprise and invited the family and the neighborhood over to see it. Jewell had baked everyone's favorite desserts and as they were enjoying the refreshments, Archie unveiled his surprise.

The short-wave radio had been invented and he had been able to get one for their house. He had it covered with a tablecloth in the living room, and when he removed the cloth, there was such a sense of excitement. Archie inquired, "Does anyone have any earthly idea what this might be?"

One of the smart mouthed kids spouted out, "Is it a lie detector machine?"

Archie had a quick retort, "Yes, and an arm will rise up out of the box and point to all of the boys and girls in the room who have told a lie to their parents."

The parents cheered wildly and the kids all looked around at each other, not knowing whether to believe him or not. Archie quickly laughed and answered with a, "No, it's not a lie detector machine, but that would be a great thing for every parent to own." He asked again, "Does anyone else have a guess?"

A shy little girl near the back timidly raised her hand and when called on, she tried to change her mind, but her mom kept encouraging her to ask her question. "You already have a phonograph on the table over there, but is it maybe a new graphophone that plays the records louder?" Her voice was so quiet that her mom had to repeat her question for her.

The adults all murmured about how smart she was to use such big words and Archie smiled at her as he answered, "That is a very good guess and I would love to have a new graphophone, but no, it is something even better than that!" The graphophone, invented by Alexander Graham Bell was a newer and improved version of the phonograph or early record player.

He turned the short-wave radio on and tuned it in and roared, "Spot on!" The sound was very static-y, but they could hear voices and Archie explained to them that he would be putting up an antenna in the backyard in order to make the sound clearer. He hoped to be able to communicate with people around the world.

Archie went on to elaborate, "Back in the year 1923 there was a successful radio connection between an operator in Connecticut and one in London. Since that time there have been several more operators with successful radio transmissions. I am joining a dozen or more amateur or 'ham' radio operators here in the United States along with about that many in Europe. We are hoping that before too much longer, we will be able to communicate with several other continents. I am planning to go to a conference designed to integrate all of our interests into one organization. Before too long, we will see a time when we are connected to our neighbors around the world!"

Many of the friends and neighbors did not understand the concepts that Archie was explaining, yet they marveled at the interest he had in so many new and exciting inventions. The family and neighbors were beside themselves. What would be the next invention?

As Jewell and Sara were finishing the cleanup in the kitchen, Sara confided to her mother, "I am really concerned about Robert. He has been so tired and run down lately."

Jewell suggested, "Why don't you let your dad and me keep the children for a weekend while you and Robert use one of the roadsters from the dealership and get away on a little trip. I bet that he is just really tired from working so hard and some time away from the kids and the responsibilities of work will be good for the both of you."

Sara mentioned her mother's idea to Robert later that evening after they had gone home and put Matt and Mary to bed. Robert agreed, but it was several weeks before they could arrange their schedules in order to be off at the same time. They headed to the mountains for rest, fresh air, and some time alone.

After returning, Robert was still not well and asked one of his partners to give him a thorough check-up. His associate asked questions and ran several tests. When the results were ready, they sat down together one afternoon to talk. The results were not good. Robert had cancer and they would try surgery and radiation. There were no guarantees that the treatment would work and his friend recommended that he take some time off to be with his family and handle his affairs. He followed his associate's advice and took a leave of absence. Sara was now using her nursing skills and her compassionate nature to tend to her ailing husband. Robert and Sara spent countless hours consoling each other and planning out how things would be for her and the children if the treatments did not help. Sara pondered to herself, *I'll probably want to move back into the house with my parents because I won't have enough money and I'll need their help with the children.* They were forced to sell their house and move back in with Archie and Jewell because Sara needed her parent's help with the children and with medical expenses. Robert's illness lingered on for several more years.

Robert felt better for a while and periodically they believed that maybe he was getting better or better yet, perhaps he was in remission. Nevertheless, they were both thankful for each day that they could spend with each other, the children, and the family.

The Porch

The Great Depression had taken a huge toll on the economy, and the town of Springfield had not been spared. Archie's dealership was selling more used cars than new, when he could sell one, and he was glad that their family had savings and each other to depend on in times such as these. His heart would break as he watched Sara tend to her frail husband in the same manner that she had tended to her dolls when she played nurse on the front porch so many years ago. She and Robert were not to have the adventures they had dreamed about for so many years. Life was not turning out the way that she had planned.

In the fall of 1930, Sara buried her beloved Robert. Matt was eight and Mary was six. They had known for a long time that their daddy was ill, but they hadn't really thought that he would die. It was the worst time that they had ever experienced. They watched as their mother cried, then they would cry, and then they would forget and want to play outside with the neighborhood children for a while.

Archie and Jewell felt as though they had lost a son as well. The town turned out for the funeral and then brought food as well as their condolences to the house. One of Robert's partners had taken Sara aside and tried to comfort her by telling several stories that had been Robert's favorites. He reminded her about the time they had double dated.

"We were picnicking and it started to pour rain. Robert yelled at you to get in the car and move it out of the dirt while the rest of us packed up the food. You tried your darndest with that old Model A, but you got frustrated with the clutch. We threw the stuff in the car and tried to push you out of what was quickly becoming a muddy sinkhole. You had your foot on the brake instead of the clutch, grinding the gears and we literally pushed the car about forty feet. We were covered in mud and you were sitting in the car, looking all fresh and dry. When Robert saw what you had done wrong, he was so mad, but later told us that he thought that you were the cutest thing he had ever laid eyes on!"

Sara laughed for the first time in days and knew that she would need to remember more of the good times that she and Robert had shared. Before her friends and loved ones left, she reminded them all of Robert's favorite quote by Robert Frost, "In three words I can sum up everything I've learned about life: It goes on."

In an effort to help the family to heal and look forward to a brighter day, Archie suggested that they spend some time sprucing up the house. Throughout the past thirty-five years, they had maintained things about the house such as the paint on the exterior and repairing the roof. Money was tight because of the Depression, but they all pitched in together and replaced the rotten wood around the exterior, trimmed trees and bushes, and gave the inside a good cleaning and a fresh coat of paint.

Sara saved most of the money from Robert's insurance policy, but announced one night at dinner that she had something that she wanted to tell the family. "Robert and I had many hours to talk about how my life would be once he died and one of the things that he hoped that I would do, would be to help with keeping this house in good condition. He loved this house and this family so very much and he wanted so badly to see the children grow up here. He asked me to pay all of the funeral expenses with his insurance money. He also asked me to make sure that I had enough money to buy the children things that they would need. Most of all, he wanted me to spend some of his money updating the kitchen. He would have wanted us to have a new electric stove and a new refrigerator."

The family laughed and cried at the same time and they all began to talk at once. Jewell cried and said, " Robert wanted to make sure that I kept on baking and cooking for his babies."

Archie announced, "Just the other day I was at the furniture store trying to work out an exchange with the owner. I was trying to figure out a way to trade him some service on his car for some new appliances. Won't he be surprised when I tell him that I can buy those appliances outright? He might even come out ahead on the deal."

Matt and Mary were up dancing around the kitchen, asking when they could have their friends over to see their new kitchen. Sara was missing Robert so much, knowing that he would have gotten so much pleasure out of this announcement and the family's excitement and laughter.

CHAPTER 12
TEN-YEAR-OLD MATT-1932

"Matt flies his imaginary planes, around the world to exciting and exotic places."

Matt had always looked like a little man and so much like his father. As he had grown taller, his face had basically stayed the same. He looked at pictures of himself as a baby, then looked in the mirror, then looked at pictures of his father and could already visualize what he would look like when he was twenty. He was born with brown eyes and a full head of dark brown hair. In spite of all that hair, he had a hard time believing that he went through a time when he was almost bald for a while.

When he was five, he had overheard some of his mother's friends comment that "he was too pretty to be a boy." He had gotten into his mother's sewing kit and had used her scissors to cut all of his hair off. She had found him sitting in the middle of a pile of chopped brown locks. She had cried for days after the barber had shaved his head so that it could grow back evenly. He had promised her that he would never cut his hair that way again, yet he knew that if he were able to be a pilot, he would have to wear it as short as possible.

The year was 1932 and Matt had been building airplanes with Tinker Toys as he patiently waited for his friend from next door to finish his homework. The day before, they had started a new adventure. They had gone on an expedition to Antarctica. It had been a beautiful Sunday afternoon and they had fantasized about another one of their heroes that they enjoyed reading about. This hero was Admiral Byrd. They had been sharing a copy of his latest book entitled *Little America*. The school librarian had borrowed a copy for them from the main library and they felt so privileged to hold it in their hands. It was a book about a camp that had been established in the Antarctic for the purpose of flying a tri-motored Ford plane to the South Pole and back. Admiral Byrd was the only man who had been to both of the poles of the world and Matt hoped that some day, he could be the first to do something equally spectacular. Admiral Byrd had flown planes since the early 1900's and had attended the United States Naval Academy and graduated in 1912. Matt secretly hoped that one day he could attend there as well. He knew that only the best and brightest students were even considered, so he studied hard in order to keep his grades high.

Ever since Matt was small, he had pretended that he was a pilot. There were pictures of him, sitting inside of a cardboard box with a propeller drawn on the front. He had spent hours in that box or many boxes that were similar. Then it was his Radio Flyer wagon. He bribed Mary to pull him fast and he would ride with his arms stretched wide. Now, at the age of ten, he placed his swim goggles over his eyes and rode his bike as fast as he could pedal. He felt the wind against his face and if he closed his eyes for a second he could almost imagine what it must feel like to be flying. His adventures were not combat adventures, but trips to see amazing and interesting places in the world that most people saw only at the movie houses. Because his parents had wanted to go to exciting places, Matt had grown up hearing and thinking about adventures far away from his backyard and this porch. For now, this was to be his pretend expedition.

Archie continued to communicate to places around the world with his short wave radio. Matt and his friend listened in when Archie had a connection. In 1933 a man named Arthur Collins founded Collins Radio Company in Cedar Rapids, Iowa. Their purpose was designing and producing short-wave radio equipment. Archie was then able to upgrade and fine-tune his own equipment. An exciting time for Archie was when Collins Radio had been able to supply the equipment used in order to communicate with Admiral Richard Byrd when he was on his 1934 South Pole Expedition. They felt as though they had an inside link into what was going on around the world. Sometimes, Matt would stay up late with his grandfather listening and learning about the world outside of his small town of Springfield.

Admiral Byrd was not the only hero that Matt had studied and mimicked with his pretend flights. The Johnson's were a husband and wife team that had met, married, and explored all around the world. Martin Johnson had been the first of the couple to explore and photograph exotic places. He had actually been part of the crew of Jack London's ship, the *Snark*, as they voyaged across the Pacific during 1907-1909. Martin met Osa in 1910, and they married and began to travel together.

When Johnny from next door bounded up onto the porch, he almost knocked Matt over with his excitement. "Let's not do Admiral Byrd this time. Can we act out the Johnsons again?"

Matt showed Johnny the plane that he had finished building and answered, "Sure. I get to be the chief this time!" He immediately got into character. "I am the chief of the Big Nambas. You will not take over our land. Our people have been in this part of northern Malekula for many a moon. You see these masks and this war paint; we eat white men that invade our land."

Johnny quickly assumed the character of Martin. "You cannot hold us hostage for long. The British will be here to release us soon! We mean you no harm. We are just taking moving pictures of you and your people." Johnny pantomimed with his hands as if he were trying to communicate with the natives that did not understand their English.

Matt interrupted and suggested, "Let's act out the part where we go back to visit."

Johnny asked, "You mean the part in the movie *Among the Cannibal Isles of the South Seas* where they go back to the land of the Big Nambas?"

"Yeah," agreed Matt, "I love that part. Let's get our bikes and ride like we're flying, then we'll land and meet with the chief."

They raced up and down the street for a while whooping and hollering, flying and soaring with the wind. Eventually they landed at the foot of the porch, ready to continue their pretend meeting with the cannibals.

Matt grabbed a stick and ran up the steps and around the corner of the porch. At the bottom of the steps, Johnny pretended to unload the plane, talking to the make-believe wife and armed escort. "You get the generator, the extension cords, the projector, and the rest of the gear. I will go and meet with the chief. Hopefully, he will remember us."

Around the corner came Matt with his spear drawn as if to attack. "You are back. What are you doing? I thought we had seen the last of you and your wife."

They stood still, eye to eye, for what seemed like eternity; the chief with his spear and his tribe, ready for attack and Martin protecting Osa, shielding her with his body. All the while the imaginary armed escort was hurriedly hooking up the generator and the projector.

Johnny shouted, "The machine will make noise, but we have something that we want to show you."

As the generator started up, the chief and the tribe shrunk back in fear, but as the movie began and the natives recognized themselves, they grew excited and hollered among themselves. "It's us. Look, that's you!"

The friends had a great time laughing and talking about seeing that movie three times. They had almost every scene memorized.

That evening as Matt lay still, waiting to go to sleep, he hoped and prayed that someday he would be able to fly a plane and travel to exotic places. He wanted desperately to create memories of his own.

CHAPTER 13
THE FOURTH OF JULY 1940

The Fourth of July celebration was on a Thursday and had to be held inside. The weather had been terrible and a lot of the relatives had not been able to make the trip. As the family added to the journals from the Treasure Chests, Matt quietly went through some of the things that were put in after his father's death and funeral. There was his dad's Bible, full of sermon notes and personal articles, a picture of Matt driving one of the new Ford Coupes from the dealership and his high school graduation diploma. His dad would have been so pleased to have watched him walk across the stage to receive it. Robert had been quite a reader and was always clipping items from the newspaper. Matt had unfolded several of them and read them. He wished that he had had more time to get to know his father better. As a child, he had taken all of their time together for granted. Along with the clippings, there was a dried flower from the graveside and other keepsakes that brought back a flood of emotions and memories of his wonderful father. As he was preparing to go off to college, it would have been a lot easier if his dad had been there to talk with him.

From across the room, Sara had been watching her son as he studied the memorabilia. She approached him and draped her arm around his shoulders.

"You miss your father, don't you?"

Matt quietly answered, "Yes, Mom, I do. He would have enjoyed this time of my life and I have so many questions that I wish that I could ask him. You're great and all, but it's guy stuff, you know what I mean?"

"I do, son, but please know that I want to be there for you whenever you need me." Sara was having trouble holding back her own emotions.

She tried to change the subject as she reached for the Japanese puzzle box and held it between her two hands. She began to twist and turn it in several directions. "I have never been able to figure this crazy thing out. Your grandfather and his gadgets. He refuses to show anyone how it works. There has got to be a way that it opens, I would imagine that it has some kind of a trap door."

She held it out to Matt, and he began to fiddle with it as he mused, "This box kind of reminds me of my life. Twists and turns, unknown answers, something there so close, but just beyond my reach. Life really is a puzzle. I guess that someday we get it open, and we find what we have been searching for."

Sara hugged her son once more, whispered, "I love you," in his ear and moved away to leave him with his thoughts.

Matt felt badly about leaving his mother and sister by themselves and it would have been comforting to have had another man to talk to about leaving home. Grandfather Archie was great and all, but his personality was different, in that he was so outgoing and talkative. That was why Grandfather Archie had been such a great salesman all of these years. Matt had the same sense of adventure, yet he was more quiet and introspective. When he tried to tell him about his fears and misgivings, Archie would laugh and say, "Son, you are the first of this family to get a chance for this great adventure. You should be excited and should be looking forward to all that life has in store for you. A famous poet, Mark Twain, once wrote, 'Confidence is the feeling you have before you understand the situation.' You are a bright young man and you can do anything that you set your mind to do." Matt hoped that Archie was right, but he was still nervous.

Years had passed since the days of wanting to go to the Naval Academy and Matt had had to change his mind about his college choice. His grades had always been good, but money was really tight. After the Great Depression, many had struggled to pay off their debts and recover from such a hard time. After the death of his father, they were still living with Sara's parents in the old family home. Matt knew that as much as everyone wanted him to pursue his dreams, he needed to be resourceful and accomplish things on his own. Besides all of that, his mother seemed really lost and helpless when they talked about him going too far away to school. He had applied and had been accepted to several colleges that were two to three hours away and finally decided on one that had a really good R.O.T.C. program. That way he could get the military training that he wanted and could possibly fulfill his dream of someday being a pilot. Matt knew that even though he felt disappointed about life, for the time being, he felt lucky that college was even an option.

In the fall of 1940, Matt said his final good-byes to his family. His grandparents were so excited for him and his mother and sister were trying to not let it show how sad they were that he would not be around every day. Thank goodness, his sister, Mary had taken a real liking to working with Archie at the Ford dealership. She said that she was going to work there part-time while she finished high school. It sure would be great to keep the business in the family.

The family waved goodbye from the porch as Matt put the last of his gear into the trunk of the sedan and he and Archie headed off to his new campus. His dreams from the front porch were becoming a reality and he had pinched himself often to see if it was really happening or was it just another one of his pretend adventures. Matt knew that he would miss his family, but they had always been able to follow their own dreams and had encouraged their children to do the same. He was determined to keep his grades high so that eventually he would be able study aeronautics. Only then would he be able to hold on to his dream of becoming a top-notch pilot.

CHAPTER 14

SARA'S ADVENTURES

"Sara wandered around in a daze for what seemed like hours before she was able to tend to her patients"

One night, not too long after Matt had left for college, Archie had asked Sara to visit him in the living room. Archie had set up a small office area in there and it was a cozy place to have private conversations. This type of visit was not unusual for Sara and her father. They had spent many evenings throughout the years discussing social and political topics. The conversations had been about the price of corn, President Roosevelt's latest projects, Europe, and the war. One night in particular, they had stayed up past midnight trying to figure out what had happened to Amelia Earhart.

This night however, the topic had not been Hitler and Stalin or any of the other news stories of the week. The topic had been about her. Archie had not wasted time with small talk. He asked, "Sara, what are you going to do with the rest of your life?"

"What do you mean, Dad?" Sara had answered his question with a question. "I have the rest of my life mapped out here in Springfield with my family."

"Sara, this was not the life that you dreamed about, it is just the one that you ended up with. What happened to the little girl who dreamed of nursing in far off lands? That was the girl who wanted to see the world."

Sara looked at her father, who she realized, knew her better than anyone. Suddenly, it dawned on her that her father was asking her questions that she didn't have answers for. She had buried many of her dreams when she buried Robert. She had felt such a huge amount of responsibility to raise the children and provide for their futures.

She thought for a while and then responded to her father, "Dad, that little girl grew up and she put away her dolls. She married, had children, became a nurse, and lost her husband. I miss Robert, but I have a good life here in Springfield."

"Yes, you do have a good life here; however I think that those dreams are still there. You have just pushed them below the surface. There is nothing that is holding you here. Matt is in college and Mary goes to school and works with me at the dealership. Your mother and I are healthy and able to check in on the children while you are away. Truth be known, they will probably spend more time looking after us." As he finished speaking he had risen to go to bed. As he was leaving the room, he made one final statement. "There is a quote from an author that I read to you when you were little. Henry David Thoreau stated, 'Our truest life is when we are in dreams awake.' All I ask is that you think about it."

As she continued to sit there for a while, what she did think about was that, as usual, her dad was right. His idea had sounded strange, but she had forgotten many of the promises that she had made to herself and to Robert before he had passed away. During the next several weeks, she spent countless hours discussing her plans with Archie. Of course, her mother was upset and made it clear that she wished Sara would stay in town and continue her own legacy of socializing with the women in town. Jewell had even tried to bribe Sara with a new car if only she would stay home. Sara had always been polite to all of her mom's friends and their daughters, but she had never related to the things that they were interested in. She hungered for adventure and when she would read of the war that was raging around the world, she wondered where she could fit into all of it.

The Porch

In 1941, war in Europe and tensions with Japan had grown. The United States had deployed more troops to the Philippines. The Army did not want to accept women directly into its ranks. The Women's Army Auxiliary Corps (WAAC) was established to work with the Army. General Marshall had believed that eventually there would be a manpower shortage, so he had helped a woman named Edith Nourse Rogers pass a bill through Congress. Women would now be allowed to work with the Army and Sara was signed up and ready to serve. She was sent to join more than one hundred nurses on the islands.

It had not been an easy decision, one that she had spent many sleepless nights praying about. Her father had helped her to carefully think through what it could mean for the future of her children if something were to happen to her. Her mother had been totally against the idea and the recruiters were concerned that she would be one of the older nurses to be sent. Thirty-one years had passed since she had pretended on the porch, but she was a determined woman and had finally set out on her long-awaited adventure.

Sara was assigned to a hospital in Manila, yet after a few days of being there, the Japanese had attacked Fort Stotsenberg, in the Philippines. Stotsenberg was located seventy-five miles north of Manila. The hospital there was not damaged, but there were many injured soldiers. The chief nurse sent some of the nurses from Manila to help out and Sara was one of them. After Christmas, they received orders to evacuate back to Manila. Two of her friends were captured during the evacuation and had been held as prisoners. Sara had hoped for adventure, but this was more than she had expected. She had missed the holidays with her children and her parents and she wondered if they would ever see her alive again. That part of the equation was a dismal thought, but as each day began, she felt an excitement that she had not felt for a very long time.

Sara wished that she could have communicated with Archie and Jewell more often. When she had first gone overseas, they had hoped to talk on the shortwave radio. A priest, Father Maximilian Kolbe had been accused of espionage because he had an amateur radio and the Germans believed that he was spying. He had been imprisoned at Auschwitz. On August 14, 1941, he had volunteered to take the place of a prisoner that was to be killed. He was canonized and declared a Martyr of Charity. As a result, all amateur radio operations were suspended. Sara and her family continued to write letters, but the delivery of them was very sporadic.

One such letter read,

March 9, 1942

Dear Dad and Mom,

I know that it has been a while since I have been able to write. I wonder how long it will take for you to get this letter and how much of it will be blacked out. I have been transferred again. This time, we were sent to the Bataan Peninsula. They have set up two hospitals there. Number 1 is for the recently wounded and Number 2 is for the soldiers that are being evacuated. I don't know how long we will stay here; there are plenty of wounded and severely hurt soldiers for us to nurse.

When I can sleep, it is for short periods of time and my dreams are full of comforting, caring for, and praying for the dying young men. I love you all and miss you terribly. Please tell the children that I am fine and that I can't wait to hold them in my arms.

Love,
Sara

There were two hospitals where Sara had been stationed. The one that Sara was assigned to had sixteen buildings. There were so many battle casualties, over 1200 in just the first month. She had never before witnessed the traumatic amputations and head, chest, and abdominal wounds. In the beginning, she had dreams of tending the soldiers, but as time continued the dreams turned to nightmares about grotesque wounds, blood, and infections. Besides the wounds from war, patients and staff suffered from tropical disease, including malaria and dysentery. Many times she thought she would faint from the sights, yet as time moved on, she was so tired that she became numb. The other hospital was for the patients that were strong enough to wait for evacuation. They were out in the open with only the shelter of a canopy of trees.

It was the end of March and Sara's hospital had been bombed. Soldiers were reinjured as the ground shook and tore apart the buildings. She recalled feeling the pressure of her head as if it were exploding. The sound was excruciating and she truly believed that her head might explode. After the attack ended, she was amazed that she was not hurt, but the scene was horrific and the air was ghastly to breathe.

Sara later recalled that she wandered around in a daze for what seemed like hours before she was able to regain her composure and get back to work. Those that had survived tried their best to carry on and tend to the injured. There was one soldier in particular that Sara felt a strong connection with. He reminded her so much of her son, Matt. The soldier was quiet and wanted more than anything in his life, to be a pilot. His dream had come true, but at what an expense. She feared that he would not survive and whenever she had extra time, she was by his bedside tending to his wounds and listening to his life story.

He was in critical shape and had a strange request for her several days before he died. He had given her his class ring and asked her to try to find his family when and if she was able to return home after the war. His name was Thomas Wayne Kirkland and he had left his son in the care of his sister when he went off to war. The son's name was Tommy Jr. and Sara promised to keep the ring safe and to look up the sister and share Thomas Wayne's last requests with her and his young son.

The war had raged on and the nurses continued to tend to the needs of the injured. Major General Wainwright was the commander of the forces on Corregidor and when it seemed that surrender to the

Japanese was inevitable, he had decided that it was time to evacuate the nurses. Sara was one of the older ones and she was ready to follow orders. She feared whether she would be able to survive if she were taken prisoner. Twenty of the nurses left the island on two Navy aircraft and her plane made it safely to Australia. They discovered after landing, that the other plane was forced to make a landing on the island of Mindanao and all aboard were taken prisoner. Some of the other nurses and a naval officer's wife safely arrived in Australia by submarine and yet, fifty-five of her fellow nurse friends were still at the base in Corregidor when the Japanese forced the surrender. She discovered in the days to follow that they were all held prisoners for three more years. Sara felt very fortunate indeed that she had not been captured. She was finished and it had been time for her to go home. She was ready! Excitement had become fear for her life and she had had more than her share. She had realized how important her family, especially her children, were to her. After she was reunited with her family, she was glad that she had been able to serve her country, but she was glad to be home in Springfield.

After returning home, she resumed her career of nursing at the local hospital. Every once in a while, she would wake suddenly, reliving one of the fearful times of the war. Sara would remind herself that she was safe, back home, in her warm bed. "Adventure – be careful what you wish for," became the motto that she reminded herself of when she became restless with her life.

In her free time, she tried to find the sister of Thomas Wayne. Her leads had all grown cold; the sister had moved several times and the sister's neighbors had lost touch with her. Sara placed the ring in a small box, with a note. Hopefully, in the future she or someone else would be able to find the soldier's family. In her free time, she wrote in her journal about her travels and her experiences throughout the war. She also hoped that the war would end before Matt would be called for duty.

CHAPTER 15
MATT'S ADVENTURES

After several years away at school, Matt had accepted an invitation to go home with a roommate for Thanksgiving. Upon arriving at their home, he had met his roommate's younger sister. Falling in love was never part of the plan for Matt's dreams, but nevertheless, it happened. Melinda was the most beautiful woman that Matt had ever seen. She had a dark complexion, brown eyes, and long, wavy brunette hair. Over the course of the next year, he and Melinda traveled between her home and his college campus. Melinda had stayed at home and was taking secretarial classes at night. She worked during the day for an accountant. As they dated and got to know each other, they realized that they shared many of the same dreams for adventure and excitement. Besides traveling and a career, she did want to have a home and a family.

Matt made it very clear from the beginning that he would always have a need for adventure in his life. He knew that being a pilot could possibly take him away from home for long periods of time. Melinda agreed that she wanted to be a part of his life, even though it meant that there would be times when she would be running their household by herself.

After graduation in May of 1942, Matt and Melinda were married and moved into the house with the porch. The wedding had been postponed several times, as they had wanted to wait for Sara to return from the war. Sara had finally returned safely and was so pleased to meet Matt's fiancé. Melinda was a beautiful young woman and it was obvious that she and Matt had a wonderful relationship. The summer was spent with Sara getting reacquainted with her parents, her children, and her new daughter-in-law. The house was crowded, but the evenings were especially fun. They spent long hours on the porch visiting and laughing about events that had happened while Matt was in school and Sara was overseas. There was always a somber atmosphere when Sara would tell about her friends that had been captured and held as prisoners of war. She would hear news occasionally that someone had died or was very ill. She realized how easily it could have been her.

In the late fall, Matt said goodbye to his new bride and the family. He had finished his training to be a pilot, had received his wings, and had requested an assignment to Asia. Before he would go to Asia, he would spend several weeks in AIT. Advanced Individual Training was required so that the new enlistees would be trained and ready when they were deployed to their stations. He had so many thoughts and bad dreams about what the Japanese had done to his mother and her friends that he wanted to see that part of the world and try to change what had happened when his mom had left there. Armed forces were still in combat and Matt wanted to do his part for his country.

Melinda had known that his career would take him away, but Asia was so far. She had confided to him one night as they got ready for bed, "I know that you need to go and I'm really proud of you and all that you have accomplished, but I sure do hope that you come home to me safely."

Matt had held her tightly and told her that he knew what he had to do, yet he would miss her terribly. "I would be lying if I told you that I wasn't scared. This is not what I dreamed of as a young boy when I dreamed of being a pilot, but this is a time of war and I need to serve my country. I'll do my darndest to come back to you safely. I love you, Melinda!"

Melinda continued her career as a secretary, but she had secretly hoped that she could one day be a bookkeeper. She was so good with numbers and as she typed letters and papers for her boss, she learned much about the business. She and Matt had even discussed the possibility of her being able to help with the war effort. When the posters featuring the character *Rosie the Riveter* were hung up at the Post Office, she had thought that maybe that would be her way to experience a part of the action. She wondered what it would be like to take one of the men's jobs on an assembly line at the local factory. Matt had helped her to understand that what she was already doing was an important part of being an American as well and that she should continue with her career. She had been glad that her days were busy. At the end of a long day, it helped if she was tired and could go to sleep quickly. If not, she would miss Matt too much. When he would write to her about his adventures, she would feel the jealousy rise up in her. She wanted some excitement in her life! Maybe in the future, she would be able to travel and see the world with Matt.

Matt was busy with his career in the Army, but as soon as he received news that Melinda was expecting their first child, he took a short leave and came home for Christmas. He knew that he would not be there when the baby was born as he was to be shipped out soon and would not be back for several months. It was a wonderful visit and the house had never looked prettier. Christmas had always been a favorite time of the year for the entire family, and there had been a steady flow of well-wishers that dropped by to see Matt and to enjoy cookies and eggnog.

When it was time for Matt to leave again, it had been even harder than the first time. As Matt stood at the curb, waving goodbye to everyone, he memorized all of the details about the scene; his wonderful family, the beautiful, twinkling Christmas tree in the front window, and the snow reflecting the sparkling of the multi-colored lights on the porch. He had to turn away and leave before he changed his mind. Would he be back? When would he be back? How different would life be?

Jake was born in the early part of 1943 and was a healthy and happy little boy. He looked just like the baby pictures of Matt, but with Melinda's beautiful dark eyes. Jake's eyes were one of his most noticeable features. Visitors often commented that they looked warm and endearing, yet at the same time were mysterious and enchanting. Those that were the closest to him were soon to realize that his eyes would reflect his personality. Even though the house was crowded, Melinda's mother was made to feel welcome and was able to come for a long visit. Melinda sent Matt letters almost every day and when she could, pictures of the baby. Matt wrote as often as possible, but his letters were censored and the details about where he was and what he was doing, were sketchy. He promised that as soon as he could, he would be home, playing with his son on the front porch.

That same year, the Japanese had closed the Burma Road. The only way to move oil, av-gas, troops, and supplies from India to the Flying Tigers in China was over the Himalayan Mountains. The mountains were so rugged that the best option was to fly the supplies in. Matt was one of the pilots chosen to fly this route that would become known as the Burma Hump. The twin-engine plane that he flew back and forth was the Curtiss C-46 Commando with a double bubble fuselage. The pilots had nick-names for the planes and as sad as it was, Matt's favorite was the "flying coffin." It was a dangerous mission involving the attacks by Japanese fighters and impossible weather with winds up to 200 mph. Many of Matt's pilot friends lost their lives flying 'the Hump'.

The planes encountered turbulence and would easily be flipped over and whipped from side to side. The view was breathtaking; an adventure that he had longed for, but the mission of 500 miles, back and forth between India and China, was a daunting challenge. As he had pretended on the front porch, he had not dreamed about the effects of the weather and the stress on his body. Flying for real was really quite different than flying in a cardboard box, in a wagon or on his bicycle. It was an exciting experience, but Matt knew that if he survived, he wanted a career where he could experience adventure with his family, out of harm's way.

CHAPTER 16
THE FOURTH OF JULY 1945

The year was 1945 and the town and the house had important anniversaries! The town was one hundred years old and was having a centennial celebration. The house was fifty years old and was also busting at the seams with excitement as it was celebrating a milestone birthday. The house had been well overdue for some major remodeling. It had been maintained through the years and newer electrical wiring and central heat had been added when they had become available. After fifty years, the exterior had needed some major paint stripped and rotten wood replaced. Boards on the porch were replaced and everything had a fresh coat of paint. The roof had been repaired before but a recent hailstorm had caused such bad damage that it was totally replaced this time.

Ever since the great Depression and the First World War, money had been tight and there were projects all around the house that needed to be addressed. Melinda had been cutting pictures out of magazines for months.

She could not wait to have the kitchen updated. Sara had told her that it would eventually be her home, so she should have the kitchen remodeled to reflect her personality. She knew that Archie, Jewell, and Sara had chosen the best appliances when they remodeled in the thirties, but the refrigerator had been fixed too many times and the door was about to come off at the hinges. The stove had cooked many delicious meals but had only two of the original four burners working, and the oven was always cooking too quickly. That was her excuse for so many of the burned meals.

The family decided to do some major work outside, as well. Besides repairing the wood and painting, they had torn down the original one car garage. It had started out as a carriage shed and then had been converted into a small garage when Archie had gotten his first Model T Ford. Since then, it had been about to fall down and had become a storage shed for old car parts, furniture, and junk from years gone by. There was enough room to build a two-car garage so that they could stop parking on the street. Lately there had been some vandalism with teenagers swinging bats at mailboxes and car mirrors. Melinda was almost more excited about getting a garage than she was her new appliances.

One would not have recognized the town. It had almost quadrupled in size, so large that now, not everyone knew each other. The Pioneer Park had been expanded to include a gazebo for a band to play and for weddings to be held during the year. There was also a road around the park that had become the Town Square. Businesses had quickly sprung up, bordering the square. A few streets over from the square, there were two new schools. Now the older children had a junior high school separated from the high school. There were several more churches than before and there were definitely more stores and restaurants. The old hotel had been remodeled and had been booked full for almost six months in preparation for the Centennial celebration.

Parades had been planned and booths had been constructed so that children of all ages would have plenty of entertainment. The Chautauqua had so many events year round and this holiday weekend had been no exception. Troops had slowly returned from their service in the war and they were to be honored in the parade. There was also a special ceremony to honor all of the loved ones that had not been fortunate enough to return home. Many of the proceeds from the booths and stores around the square were going to be used to erect a memorial for the fallen soldiers from Springfield.

On July 4th, a sense of excitement and expectancy was in the air. Red, white, and blue decorations were everywhere and store windows sported "Welcome Home" posters. The forty-eight star "Old Glory" waved in almost every yard and Victory gardens, planted several years before were full of fresh vegetables. The war had ended in Europe in May and hopefully the fighting in Japan would be over soon as well. The town and all of America were ready to get back to a normal life, whatever that was. Gas rationing and food coupons were soon to be no longer necessary and it was hard to remember what life was like before wartime. Sara had put a rock from Corregidor, maps and postcards from Manila, and a fan from China into the Treasure Chests. She had written a journal telling about her near death experiences which she also included. Matt had maps from Burma and there was a picture of him standing by the plane that he had flown.

This year, Matt was especially curious about the Japanese puzzle box that no one seemed to know anything about. He realized that in the past, his grandfather Archie had watched as he turned it over and over, studying it, and wondering how to get it open. Later on, in the evening when Archie and Matt were left alone to visit on the porch, Archie addressed the subject of the Treasure Chests, which now consisted of two crates. He had long before shared with Sara the importance of keeping journals and timelines of the family's histories so that future generations would be able to continue the legacy that Archie had started many years before.

"Matt, I've been waiting to tell you about some of the interesting things that are included with all of the memorabilia." Archie had also planned on telling Matt about moving the safe and placing it in his bedroom closet. He also thought that someone should know how to open the Japanese puzzle box.

Melinda stuck her head out the door and interrupted, "Matt, Jake is ready for his bedtime story. You promised to tuck him in after he had his bath. Sorry, Archie. Can you all talk later?"

This conversation would have to be continued at a different time. Maybe Sara had already told Matt that she had put the ring and some other papers in the safe as well. Archie was starting to have trouble remembering if the conversations that were in his head were real conversations that he had had with others. Ever since Jewell had passed away a year ago, he caught himself forgetting things that had happened and things that he had already told people.

CHAPTER 17
THE BERLIN AIRLIFT

"During the Berlin Airlift, adults waited for food and supplies and the children looked skyward, watching for the parachutes filled with candy"

After Matt had returned home from the war he had been able to get a job flying for a major airline. He would be gone one or two nights a week, but most of the time, he was home and able to help Melinda with Jake. One day, between flights, Matt answered the phone and heard a familiar voice on the other end. It was his squadron commander that had been in charge when Matt and the others in his battalion had flown the Burma Hump. Matt heard uneasiness in the commander's voice as he began to tell about a special assignment that would require Matt's services.

The war had ended before Matt had completed his tour of duty and he was listed as a reservist. He had known that he could be called back up at any time, but so far the Cold War had been about democratic countries versus communism in Europe. Matt had listened intently when the news featured President Truman discussing the conditions in central Europe. The war had certainly wrecked havoc on the countries that had been bombed. Millions of people had died and the towns and villages were suffering from numerous hardships. Communism had started to spread and in 1947 Truman had presented the Truman Doctrine. The Doctrine stated that the United States would make every effort to help all countries fight communism. Secretary of State George Marshall had announced plans to help rebuild Europe and get money into their economies again. The Soviets had been invited to be included, but Stalin, their leader, had turned down the offer.

The commander had recapped all of this information to Matt and then came to the part that Matt would be involved in. The Soviet Union had decided that it did not want the help of the Allies and would set up a blockade around Berlin and its people. The children and adults needed fuel, food, and necessities. The railways and roads were barricaded so that the only way in was by air. Matt had survived the Burma Hump and had proven to be a great pilot, so his services were once again required. That evening, Matt shared with Melinda that their life was going to have some more adventure. She cried and held him tightly. "I will miss you even more this time. I don't want to sound selfish, but I can't raise Jake on my own. Your mom has shared so much with me about how hard it was for her to raise you and Mary by herself."

Matt held her close and assured her, "They will not be firing on us this time. This mission is called Operation Vittles and these children and adults need food. This time I will be flying the C-47 Skytrain. It is a much larger plane capable of carrying 3.5 tons of cargo. The danger will be the flying and the long hours. I promise that I will be as careful as I can be. My life is with you and our family, here in Springfield, and I'll be home as soon as I finish my duty to my country."

From June of 1948 to May of 1949, Matt and many other pilots carried over 13,000 tons of supplies and food daily into Berlin. The United States Air Force, Royal Air Force, and the Commonwealth nations provided the planes, pilots, and supplies. The success of the airlift was humiliating to the Soviets and they eventually lifted the blockade. Matt and Melinda had not known going into the mission that it would last less than a year, but it was quite a relief when he was, once again, home safely.

One of the stories that he had enjoyed telling for years to come was about the "Candy Bomber." One of the other airlift pilots named Lt. Gail Halvorsen had noticed the Berlin children as they would watch with excitement as the planes would fly over and land with the supplies. The Lieutenant had a brilliant idea one evening when he was thinking about his own children back home. He bought out all of the candy from the commissary where he was based and in the evenings, would tie it into small bundles with small strips of cloth. He would then drop the small parachutes to the children; imagine their excitement. His "Operation Little Vittles" caught on and in no time, other pilots were joining in. They started by giving him their rations of chocolate, candy, and chewing gum along with their handkerchiefs. Before long, tons of candy and gum already assembled into mini parachutes had been sent from the states. Many of the pilots dropped the parachutes and by the end of the airlift, over 100,000 children had received an extra dose of sweetness from the American pilots.

CHAPTER 18
TEN-YEAR-OLD JAKE-1953

"Jake reads on the porch as he watches for Johnny the mailman and the Bookmobile"

Jake was a dark-complexioned boy. He was small for his age and his posture was not erect as he struggled to get comfortable in his wheelchair. His dark hair was cut neatly and he was well groomed. His ears seemed a little large for his face as if he had not yet grown into them or they had grown faster than his head. He had brown eyes like his father, but his features were more like his mother's side of the family. He was dressed warmly in a pullover sweater because in the shade of the porch with the breeze blowing, he had a tendency to get chilled. The polio epidemic had reached its peak the year before and the figures had been staggering. Almost fifty-eight thousand cases in one year alone. Even though the years following the Second World War had been considered America's golden age of opportunity, there were still serious concerns to deal with. Communism, the threat of nuclear war, and polio were tops on the lists of issues that Americans had to worry about. Jake was one of three children in Springfield that had contracted polio and the community was not sure how they would react to his situation and the other children with this affliction.

Matt and Melinda had faced many obstacles in their life when Jake had become infected with the dreaded polio. He had been so healthy one day and sick the next. As a baby, he had learned how to crawl, pull up, and then walk, right on schedule. One morning, as Melinda had lifted Jake out of his highchair and tried to put him on the floor, his legs had buckled under him. At first Melinda thought that he was being silly with her. "Jake, honey, stand up for mommy." She tried once again to stand him on the floor. "Jake, stand up!" He cried because her voice had sounded so impatient. She plopped him on the floor and thought that he would just crawl off to play. He continued to whimper and she reached down and picked him up. She carried him over to a chair and sat with him for a while in her lap. He felt warm to her and she wondered if he was still sick from his tonsillitis that he had had two weeks before.

She remembered it as if it was just the other day. She had read a short book to him, thinking that she would try to put him down again after he had been distracted for a while. He seemed so peaceful in her arms. It was not time for his nap, yet he was so relaxed. She decided that he needed to play some by himself while she cleaned up the kitchen. She watched from the kitchen as he scooted himself closer to his toys. He was still whining and whimpering some. She knew as well as everyone, what the symptoms of polio were. She called Matt, "Matt, there is something wrong with Jake! I can't get him to stand up! I'm going straight to the doctor's office."

Matt promised to meet her there as soon as he could get there. "I love you, Melinda. Please be careful driving. I know what you are thinking, but it may be nothing."

It was as bad as they had both dreaded. Jake had contracted polio. No one really knew how it happened; yet the muscles deteriorated as if they were dissolving. It had been the scariest ordeal of their lives. He ran a high fever and seemed to ache from his head to his feet. The doctor came to their house because no one knew for sure who would come down with it next.

For the time being, it seemed to be his legs, but they had been so afraid that it would affect his entire body. Melinda remembered that Jake had been sick with an ear infection along with his tonsillitis and they soon learned that polio was contagious. While his immune system was weak, he had probably contracted it. As hard as it was to learn to cope with the community's reaction and the fear of spreading it to other friends and relatives, they felt fortunate that he was alive, seemed to have most of his paralysis below his waist, and would not need to use an iron lung. An iron lung was necessary when a person needed a type of ventilator to help with breathing. The muscle quality of one leg was worse than the other and they soon reconciled themselves to the fact that he would probably not ever walk again.

Jake had once again been watching a pair of doves prance about the front yard. They were not even afraid of him anymore; they had gotten so used to him being on the porch. After they had flown away, the squirrel that he had named Bushy, scampered up on the porch, and nibbled on a nut as if he was showing off his newest treasure. These animals had become Jake's entertainment on the days when the weather was nice and he could soak up some sunshine. The postman, Johnny, had been walking his route and Jake noticed him sorting the mail before he would get to each house. Jake was hopeful that there would be a new issue of his *Boy's Life* magazine and his package containing the "Secret Signalscope" that he had ordered from the *Sky King* Radio Premiums. His last issue of the magazine was falling apart from being read and reread and the toy was at least a week late in coming – he sure hoped that he hadn't wasted fifteen cents.

Sometimes, Johnny would stop and visit with the people walking by or working in the flowerbeds. Jake glanced at his watch. It was a game he would play with himself. How long would it take Johnny to get to their house?

Johnny was right on schedule, as usual, and asked, "Jake, how are you feeling today?"

He replied, "I am having a pretty good day. I had my therapy this morning, so I am tired, but it is too nice of a day to stay indoors." His therapist, Sue, had told him that he had done really well with his exercises. Ever since he had contracted polio, he had someone come by almost every day to help him with his leg exercises and his muscle tone. He was sitting in what was his third wheelchair. He had either out grown them or they had worn out.

Jake was watching as Johnny folded the mail to hand it to him. "Johnny, you're killing me with excitement. Did I get my radio premium today? Did I get my magazine?"

"Yes, you did. Both things." Johnny couldn't string him along any longer. "You better be eating some more Peter Pan Peanut Butter so that you can order something else. *Sky King* comes on again Saturday morning and I bet that there will be a new toy to start saving for."

Johnny had stayed around long enough to talk about the latest book that Jake was reading. It was about Franklin Delano Roosevelt and his presidency, his trials and tribulations, and the obstacles that he had overcome. Jake had decided from the first book that he had read about Roosevelt, that *he* was his hero. The lady from the bookmobile, Sally, had been able to find some extra books for him to read. The bookmobile had been added as an extension of the public library. Their family's Ford dealership had helped the school district with funding for the bookmobile that was built on a Ford chassis. So many of the children at the elementary school were not able to go down to the library at the square to check out books and their school didn't have a library for their use. The bookmobile went by the school weekly and had set up a plan whereas Sally would also come by Jake's house once a week. Jake was especially eager on these days because he enjoyed Sally's company and he was always ready for new books.

Franklin D. Roosevelt had died in office, shortly after his fourth term had begun. Harry Truman, his vice-president, was forced to take up where FDR had left off. Many had known that President Roosevelt had polio, but did not know the extent of his paralysis. The press had been careful to not photograph him in his wheelchair and when he spoke in public his aides had helped him to rise to the podium. His fireside chats to the American public were delivered over the radio so he was seated and not seen. What Jake admired about the President's resolve was that he did not want his disease to limit his life. He had contracted polio in 1921 at the age of thirty-nine, almost as suddenly as Jake had contracted it. Throughout his life in politics, Roosevelt was able to be influential in promoting the fight against polio.

In 1938, a comedian, dancer, singer, and songwriter named Eddie Cantor had suggested a plan for a fundraising campaign that would fund the National Foundation for Infantile Paralysis. He called his campaign The March of Dimes. During the Christmas season booths were set up and children were encouraged to donate a dime to the cause. They could also send them through the mail, and the dimes had poured into the White House. Jake had actually benefited from the March of Dimes because part of his wheelchair and therapy costs had been paid for by the foundation. Each time that he would spot a dime, with Roosevelt's face, he thought about the importance that one person could make on so many other's lives. Jake had many favorite quotes from FDR, but his favorite that he quoted often was, "The only thing that we have to fear, is fear itself."

His dad had told him as many stories as he could remember about Roosevelt and his mom could remember writing a book report about Eleanor, Roosevelt's wife. Both Roosevelt and his wife had done so much to help people with disabilities and that was what was so intriguing to Jake. Unlike many other children his age, he had known exactly what he wanted to do when he grew up. He wanted to study hard, make good grades, and go to law school. As a lawyer, he would be able to work on making things equal for all people, no matter what their limitations were. He had been left out of so much and wanted life to be different for others. He remembered the pain and frustration of not being able to go to school because there were no ramps. There were not enough aides and teachers to help him to get around. Changing classes, getting to lunch, and using the restroom would have been impossible. Of course, the teachers came to him and he was able to keep up, but it was just not the same. He wanted to sit in a classroom, raise his hand when he knew an answer, and take tests with the others. He wanted to laugh and tell jokes with the other guys at the cafeteria table. He wanted to feel as normal as possible. He knew that if he could go to law school and become a lawyer, he would try hard to make life fair for others. He could envision a future where disabled people could go and do anything that they set their minds on.

The next morning when Johnny brought the mail by, Jake was obviously excited about something. Jake waited until Johnny was within earshot and then began to spew information.

"You would not believe what I am going to get to do this next weekend. You know I've been scouting with the Cub Scouts for several years, but have never been on a campout. Dad and my leaders have figured out all of the details so that I can go and be a real part of the troop. Obviously, I can't do everything like tug of war and digging the latrine, but I can help pitch my tent, build a fire, and work on my outdoor badges. They just lowered the age for being in Boy Scouts – used to be twelve and now it's eleven. One more year and I can wear a Boy Scout uniform and work on more badges!"

Johnny said, "I never realized that you hadn't been on a campout. I knew that you went to the banquets and badge ceremonies and I remember you building and racing your car in the first Pinewood Derby, but you have never spent the night?"

"No," Jake replied, "I have never spent the night away from home. Mom is worrying about the silliest details, but my dad will be there to help get me in and out of my wheelchair. I can't wait to cook over an open campfire, eat smores and tell ghost stories. I have some doozies—they won't be able to sleep without having nightmares."

Johnny just laughed and said, "That's great, you are going to have so much fun; can't wait to hear all about it. I better get going. See you tomorrow, Jake."

Jake did go camping and had a great time. As he got older, he camped a lot and was able to go through Boy Scouts, the Explorer Program, and also the God and Church Program. One of his den leaders, Mr. Ernest Palmer, Jr., made sure that Jake had as many opportunities as possible. He had been in WWII as a Navy Seal. He was also a lawyer, a state representative and was in the Rotary Club. Jake could not have known how much of his future was being molded by the fun that he was having during his time in scouting and the people that he was being influenced by.

Two years had passed, the year was 1955 and Matt was sitting on the porch, rocking his new son, Mike. He had beautiful red, curly hair, a temperament to match and could squall loud enough for the neighbors to hear. Jake was now twelve, and like his father loved to spend countless hours on the porch. Matt had been gone most of Jake's younger years and lately Jake had enjoyed having his father around. Matt had become a commercial pilot and, now, it was very seldom that he was gone for more than a day or two. Jake had heard the stories and seen the pictures of his father pretending to be a pilot on this very porch. Jake's imaginative play had been limited to reading about others and their conquests of life. His social life was with friends that he had in his scout troop. He had known that his time on the porch would hold a different type of legacy for the family and even though he felt trapped in the wheelchair, he still had dreams and goals and was ready to be a part of society.

Mary had continued to help her grandfather, Archie, at the Ford dealership and as he had slowly eased into retirement, she had been willing to take over. The people in town had slowly gotten used to a woman business leader in their midst and the social skills that she had learned from her grandmother, Jewell, had paid off in ways that none of them would have ever imagined. The dealership was starting to thrive as many in town were able to afford one or more cars per family. The Ford Fairlane, Thunderbird, and Crown Victoria were some of the more popular family cars and the F100 with a new chrome grille and matching parts was the dream of every high school young man.

The next year, Archibald had passed away in his sleep. The doctor had determined that his heart had just worn out. He had seemed tired a lot, but he *was* ninety-one. Each day for Archie was different. One day he felt good enough to head downtown to the bank and eat lunch at the diner, and the next day, he took two naps. Another day he might wander around the house looking for Jewell and later that evening he could tell a story from the 1920s and not skip a detail. The family had been glad that Melinda was able to handle her bookkeeping job from home and could be there if he needed someone. Shortly thereafter, Sara had passed away from a severe respiratory infection. She had had breathing problems since the war and every time that she fell ill, it became harder and harder for her to recover. The family had suffered two losses in a brief period of time and having a toddler around was a nice diversion.

Melinda's younger sister, Bonnie, and her husband had moved to Springfield after they had married. Bonnie's first child, named Scott was born in 1944. Scott and Jake had played together on the porch until Jake contracted polio. After that, Bonnie was afraid to bring Scott over, so they had not grown up as close cousins. Three months after Mike was born, Bonnie and her husband gave birth to their second son and named him Brandon. Both families had worried about the polio, but were hoping that the vaccinations that all of the children had received would keep them safe. As Mike and Brandon grew up together, they were always playing together on the porch.

CHAPTER 19
TEN-YEAR-OLD MIKE-1965

Mike had a rough, ruddy look to his skin. He had had scrapes and bruises all over his body for most of his life. He was all boy and not afraid of anything. His mom, Melinda, always said, "Mike learned how to climb before he walked. I can't tell you how many times I rescued him from the back of that sofa or grabbed him off of the countertop as he tried to find cookies in the cabinets." He and Jake had many fun times together even though Jake was confined to a wheelchair. Mike thought that the chair was another one of his play toys and had learned how to walk using the wheelchair as his walker. Jake loved the times that his mom had put he and Mike on the floor to play blocks, wrestle, or watch TV together.

Today, Mike and Brandon had run home from school, challenging each other to see which one was the fastest. Mike got to the porch first, and hollered, "Won! I have to go in and change. Meet you in five."

Brandon slowed down, determined that he was going to win next time and hollered back over his shoulder, "Don't start without me."

Mike changed into his frayed jeans that were way too short. He was glad to see that he was finally growing; he was tired of feeling shorter than Brandon. He told his mom about his day and answered all of her usual questions about homework and school. He grabbed a banana and some cookies and accidently let the door slam as he went out to put on his crummy shoes that were on the porch. He could hear his mom yell the usual, "Don't slam the door."

His shoes had holes on the top, knotted, broken laces, and most of the soles were rubbed bare. He laughed to himself and said, "These ought to be called my brake shoes. They're my built in stops for my bike and my skateboard." He remembered with a grimace about the broken arm that had just finished healing. His "brakes" hadn't worked so well and he had wiped out big time on his skateboard. Six weeks was a long time for a cast. The only good thing about it had been that he had gotten a lot of attention and hadn't been able to work very hard on his homework. His handwriting had never looked very neat, and he had an excuse for a while, until he built up the strength in his wrist again.

As cousins, Mike and Brandon were more like best friends. They were inseparable.. If you looked closely, you could have seen the similarities in the boys eyes and mouths. Standing side by side was a different story. They looked as different as night and day. Brandon was taller by about a head and was a stockier build. If they had not always been outside running around, he would have been too heavy for his age. He had sandy, brown hair with a cowlick that made it stick up in the back. The front of his hairline had what was called a widow's peak, yet he hated for anyone to call it that.

There was a time in the second grade when he came home from school with a black eye because he had fought an older boy at recess. Brandon had not known that his hair looked any different from anyone else's until the older kids started calling him "girl hair." He had shoved this third grader who proceeded to teach him a lesson. Lucky for both of them, the teachers had not noticed when they lined up to go in. His dad had given him a long lecture about letting other kids bug you and fighting at school.

They did everything together, every day, every evening, and every weekend. Mike was three months older than Brandon, but Brandon had just had his tenth birthday, so they were now the same age again. Mike loved it when for three months he could brag that he was older. Mike had gotten a skateboard for his birthday and Brandon had hoped for one also. Up until birthday time, they had shared Mike's; taking turns and trying all sorts of moves. Now that Brandon had his own, they were able to practice together.

Mike and Brandon had seen a movie preview at the Plaza Theater about surfing. They could not wait for *The Endless Summer* to be released. They were already saving their money so that they could see it over and over again. Their dreams were to head to the beach and be the best surfers ever. They would take their skateboards over to the hill by the reservoir and fly down the one way road, pretending that they had caught the big one. It was worth every scraped knee, bruised ankle, and broken arm.

Other times, they would use the handicap ramp in the front of the house. It was a little steep for them to pretend that they were surfing the perfect wave, but it made for some really great runs. Sometimes they even put on their bathing suits pretending that they had wetsuits. With their hair slicked back they would holler, "Surf's up! Here's a gnarly one." Some of the other boys in the neighborhood would ride their bikes by and laugh at their shenanigans, but Mike and Brandon didn't care. They knew what they wanted to do as soon as they were old enough. The movie was going to be about two buddies that traveled the world, searching each and every beach for the perfect wave. As they daydreamed about the future, they would talk about exotic places that had wonderful beaches and awesome waves.

Today, they sat for a while, finishing their snacks and talking about the adventure that they wanted to pretend about. They were thumbing through the *Surf Guide Magazine* that Jake had given Mike for his birthday. Mike suggested, "Let's pretend that we are in Hawaii, we have paddled out to the line-up and are waiting for a swell."

"Yeah," Brandon replied with his mouth so full that he almost choked on his snack.

They pretended to swim out far into the ocean to where the reef allowed them to almost stand and watch the waves. Mike hollered over the deafening sound of the waves, "What about this one?"

Brandon hollered back, "No, not big enough."

They pretended to tread water for a while and then they spotted it at the same time. "Here it is. Let's go." They headed out, one at a time, speeding down the ramp, down the front walk, across the bare dirt that was once the yard, and down the sidewalk until they hit the uneven patch of concrete that was their beach. They collapsed in a fit of laughter, rolling off of their boards, shouting and high-fiving about the awesome wave that they had just surfed off of the coast of Oahu.

"Could life get any better?" Mike wondered aloud. "It will be awesome."

As time went on, Mike tried to concentrate on life other than traveling the world and surfing, but he was so intent on this one thing. His older brother, Jake, had studied hard all the way through school. Jake was smart; he finished high school and then college. He had always wanted to be a lawyer and he had applied and been accepted into law school. The family was so proud of Jake and his accomplishments and at the dinner table, the conversation usually ended up with either Matt or Melinda trying to convince Mike that he should be planning on going to college as well. Many a meal, Mike would eat with his head staring down at his plate, listening, and not arguing with his parents. He had thought, *That sounds really neat for Jake, but Brandon and I are a team, and we have plans that don't include college. Why go to college when travel and adventure could be looming on the horizon?*

CHAPTER 20
THE FOURTH OF JULY 1972

The family was once again gathered for the family reunion and the Treasure Chests now consisted of several crates of keepsakes. Many in the family had continued to keep notes and rosters of the family members, birthdays and deaths on a family tree and where everyone was living. It sure had made it easy to know each year, that the reunion was held on the Fourth of July. This year, Matt and Melinda had bought Slinkys. The toy had been invented in 1943 by Richard James, but had become popular recently because of the jingle: "A Wonderful toy, It's fun for a Girl and a Boy." The children had a great time playing with them on the porch and the steps of the house.

In 1972, the Fourth was on a Tuesday and there had been an extra long weekend. The family had lots of time to visit, eat, and enjoy the festivities at the Town Square. The newest gadget around was the Swinger Camera by Polaroid and they took pictures of each family and every escapade that the kids could pose for.

There would be more picture memories in the Treasure Chests than ever before.

As the children played, the others sifted through the memorabilia that was laid out on the tables. Matt picked up the items one by one, and as he handled the Japanese puzzle box, he casually commented, "Has anyone ever figured this thing out?

"I have spent hours with that thing. I love a good puzzle, but that thing just frustrates the fire out of me." Jake continued, "I think that great-grandfather secretly hoped that one of us kids would have played with it long enough to get it open, but believe me when I say that I tried."

Mike chimed in, "Maybe when Brandon and I are surfing around the world, we can find someone that has some experience with those types of puzzles and give us some clues. There might actually be some kind of hidden treasure in there and we could all be rich."

"Yeah, right. You wish that life was that easy. Open this small puzzle box and out pops a genie that grants you three wishes." His mom tried to be funny, but she worried that Mike was always looking for an easy way out, and she knew that life was not always easy.

Mike and Brandon had wanted to ride their skateboards in the parade, but had opted to ride on the football team float. They had gone through all of the keepsakes in their rooms and had decided to put some of their extra stuff in the crates. There were pictures of them on their skateboards and maps, marked with beaches around the world that they wanted to surf. Included were news articles about the Apollo 16

Mission and Watergate. They had double-dated to almost every dance and they included pictures. Ticket stubs, spirit ribbons, football programs, they had shared it all. Life was full of special memories that could never be forgotten or repeated.

The boys had had another one of their arguments. They had been playing together for seventeen years and for many of those years they had dreamed of traveling, bumming around, and surfing together. Recently, they hadn't agreed on their future plans. Brandon had started this argument and had casually commented, "I think some of the dreams we used to have about being beachbums, were kind of dumb. Whatever made us think we could just pack up the car and head to the beach, blaring our 8 track tapes with the windows rolled down?"

There was silence for a long time as Mike had thought about how mad he had gotten just the other day when they had tried to have this same conversation. Finally, he responded, "We've planned all our lives for this time in our life. We always talked about how all of the older people around us seem so old and tired all the time. We agreed that we were going to be different." He paused for a second and then continued, "I want to do something different, something that no one else in this family has ever done. I want freedom and I want to surf…with or without you."

There, it had been said. Brandon turned away so that Mike couldn't see the hurt in his eyes. He had been talking with his mom and dad about going to college and he had hoped that he and Mike could have talked about their futures without arguing. They had been best friends for their entire lives, but their lives had had many differences. They were looking at their futures through different perspectives. As the silence had continued, they had both wondered what their senior year would be like. Football? Girlfriends? Prom? Would they share these memories together or begin separate journeys?

Brandon's brother, Scott, had been to Vietnam. He had been one of the lucky ones to come home alive, even though he had lost the use of part of his arm and hand. His squad had stumbled onto a minefield and the explosion had killed several of his fellow soldiers. His arm was severely injured, but in spite of the excruciating pain that curled through his body, he had helped to drag three of the injured soldiers to safety. As enemy fire continued to erupt around them, the wounded had hidden in the jungle for hours before they were rescued. He had only been home for six months and seemed very bitter and felt that society owed him something. The town had had a parade when he returned. His Bronze Star given for bravery and heroism and his Purple Heart given for being wounded in combat had been on display at the high school.

Scott had been treated like a hero at first, but after time many had forgotten him and why he had fought. He was back at home living with his mom and dad, trying to hold down a part-time job. Brandon had watched while his family had coped with Scott's disability. He felt as if he was supposed to grow up quickly and think more seriously about his future. Maybe he should be doing something more than surfing around the world.

He now felt the urge to get an education and make something of himself. He also knew that Scott had not had an opportunity to go to college and now had trouble finding a good job.

On the other hand, Mike had watched his older brother, Jake, struggle with polio his entire life. He had sensed that life was really difficult for a person with disabilities. Jake had worked really hard and had finally finished college and then law school. He was so determined to make a difference for a cause that he believed so strongly in. When he was home for the holidays, he would talk endlessly about disabled people and how there needed to be legislation for their protection. Mike had listened to all of these conversations and wished that he could escape. Life was too serious, too depressing, and too much work. He thought to himself, *I can't wait to graduate from high school, pack my truck, and get out of here.* Mike had secretly wished that Scott and Jake had been just regular brothers so that life had not gotten so complicated. He began to spend most of his free time on the porch daydreaming about surfing and bumming around on his own. He also got out his old sketchpads that he had used throughout the years. He had more free time without Brandon around and he had gone back to drawing. Funny, how his plans and dreams had gotten so messed up.

CHAPTER 21
THE ACCIDENT

"Mike loves his freedom in Hawaii, but is devastated about the accident after he calls home"

Two years had passed and in 1974, Mike called to check in with his mom and dad. In Hawaii, he worked more than he played. It was so expensive to do anything there, yet he loved his life. No one was there to tell him what to do or where to go. He called on a Friday evening, hoping that everyone would be at home, but the minute the phone was answered, he knew that something was wrong. His mom tried to talk to him, but started to cry.

His dad took the phone and asked, "Where are you?"

"I'm in Hawaii, the same place I've been for the last year." He knew that he shouldn't be smart talking to his dad, but he hadn't been able to help himself. He knew that something was wrong and that he should have been checking in more often. He had lost track of time and had been so busy with his life, plus it was really expensive to call.

"Mike, this is going to be hard to hear, but Brandon has been in an accident." Matt paused to let the news sink in. "He and some friends were coming home from an out-of-town football game and had a wreck."

Mike interrupted his father, "He's going to be okay isn't he?"

Matt replied hesitantly, "No, he didn't make it. The police think that they were all killed instantly."

"Dad, tell me this is a joke. This can't have happened. What do I do?" Mike was in disbelief as the news settled in.

"Mike, we tried to figure out a way to find you, but you didn't call and we didn't know how to reach you."

Mike asked again, "Dad, what should I do?"

Matt responded with a quiet, "I don't know what you can do. We are all still in shock around here and the family is trying to deal with it, the best that we can."

They hung up after a while, Mike giving his dad a mailing address and promising to call soon.

Mike went back to his apartment. He cried for a long time and threw a few things against the wall.

The Porch

If only Brandon had come with him, this would not have happened.

It took several months for Mike to get his mind sorted out. He felt that he was living in a nightmare that he couldn't wake up from. His mother had sent him the article from the *Springfield Daily* and he scoured it trying to envision how the accident had happened. Brandon had driven a carload of guys from his college dorm to the out-of-town game. They had driven back late at night. The drunk driver had run a red light and had hit them. They had all been killed instantly.

Mike had been trying to live a dream for Brandon and himself and it wasn't fun anymore. He found himself basically going through the motions of life and he felt really sad and old. He now understood some of what his cousin had felt when he came home from Vietnam. The only difference was that Scott had served his country and was partially handicapped. Mike had served himself and lost his cousin. What had he accomplished? He sold off his belongings and his surfboards and finally had enough money for the plane ticket home. Not even twenty years old and Mike was forced to give up the dream that he had spent most of his life dreaming about.

CHAPTER 22

THE FOURTH OF JULY 1974

The summer of 1974 was a really low point in Mike's life. He felt lost and had a hard time getting excited about anything or anyone. He had helped his mom and dad get ready for the reunion, but his heart wasn't in it. He had put a shell necklace from Hawaii into the Treasure Chests along with some baseball cards that he and Brandon had traded and collected together. Jake had cleaned out some of his own things and had placed his academic letter from college alongside of a copy of his diploma. Scott had put the citations that went with his medals that he received for his service in Vietnam. As Mike, Jake, and Scott exchanged stories about the past couple of years and how it all compared to their memories of playing and pretending on the porch, they agreed that being young and carefree was the best time of one's life.

That next fall, Mike threw some used furniture and a few belongings in the back of an old '65 Ford pickup truck that he had bought after saving his money all summer. As he pulled away from the old house, out of habit he shoved an old Beach Boys cassette into the built-in 8-track tape player and began to reminisce. He had come home and gotten a job at the local hardware store. Living under his parent's roof had been just about unbearable, but it had taken a while to get things in his mind sorted out. Life had gotten really complicated and he had finally decided what he had to do. He and Brandon had always been so close and in his heart, he wanted to do something to honor Brandon, so he was going off to college. He had no idea what he wanted to study, but there would be plenty of time to decide on that in the future. Mike had quickly realized that just because you made plans didn't mean that they always worked out the way that you expected. He had been completely out of money so he had taken out a loan and had made plans to live in a boarding house with some other young men. It turned out to be an adventure that he would have never imagined for himself.

The guys at the boarding house ended up being great guys. They had all lived some really interesting lives and after they had all settled into a routine, they opened up about their pasts and what had led them to this point in their lives.

At mid-term, they decided to rent a house together. It was in pretty bad shape, but Mike had worked at the hardware store long enough to learn a little bit about tools and woodworking. He had never minded working with his hands and before long, he and the other guys were fixing up the old house. The landlord was impressed with the improvements that they were making and he started to deduct some of their rent and also paid for some of the materials. Little did Mike know then, that in the near future, he would need to be making repairs and remodeling his old childhood house and porch. He was gaining valuable experience for future projects.

CHAPTER 23
THE PROJECT

Mike had been off to school for a few years and had really enjoyed college more than he would have ever imagined. The first couple of semesters, he had taken basic courses. In 1977, as the third year began, he took a marketing class that opened up a whole new world for him. The class was assigned a project and told that they could choose a partner to work with. John, one of the guys that he lived with, had become a good friend and was in his class. They decided to work on the project together. They had learned from the very beginning that they shared some of the same interests growing up. They had both enjoyed skateboarding and had both done some surfing. Recently they had been playing hockey at the college gym. They had a lot of fun together and knew that they would make a good team. They began to brainstorm about their project together. They were to invent a product, research and develop it, plan for manufacturing it, and market it. It was a huge project that would take up the entire semester and be most of their grade. Little did they know it would turn into quite a future for the both of them.

They had spent several days tossing around ideas and then one night when they were reminiscing about their childhood, they came up with an idea. They talked about the years that they had spent skateboarding and decided that they would feature a product that had not been manufactured yet. Research showed that back in 1759, a Belgian violinist had attached wooden spools to the front and back of a pair of shoes so that he could mimic ice-skating at a costume party. He had crashed into a mirror and been laughed at, but eventually roller skates had become popular.

Mike and John thought that they could combine the concepts of a roller-skate and an ice skate and make a new type of skate. They sketched and sketched and came up with a drawing of what they would refer to as a line-a-roller. It would look like a pair of roller-skates with wheels in a line. They laughed about how it was such a simple idea and yet no one had thought of it before. They found some information about inline skates being experimented with a few times in Europe, but no one in the United States had patented the product.

They were on to the manufacturing phase of their project. Mike and John found that there were several companies that could manufacture the shoe part of the skate and they both had experience with the different wheels that they had had on their skateboards. They contacted a company that made their favorite brand of wheels and soon they were on their way to proposing a way to manufacture the product. Marketing for the product would be easy. Boys of all ages would love a new toy. The thrill of speeding down the sidewalk or a road with a type of ice-skating or roller-skating rhythm would be such a rush. They could be used in all types of weather and in many locations. While they were working out the details about the shoe designs and colors, they realized that girls could use them as well. Skateboarding had been mainly a boy's sport, but now boys and girls could hang out together and their market would double. This would be such a great alternative to riding bikes and so much easier for someone to take this sports equipment with them. Their project was sure to be a winner.

The class project had gone well and the professor had been impressed with all of their hard work.

During the marketing part of the product, Mike had discovered the love of his life. He and John had consulted with a student, freelance artist to help with the marketing campaign part of their project. Donna was very knowledgeable and they had been impressed with her talents and expertise. She was quiet and very adept at what she suggested to them. Each time that she presented ideas to them, Mike noticed that she would study his face carefully. In the beginning, he thought that she was searching for reactions to her proposals, but after a while, he realized that she was interested in him as a person. They quickly became friends and in due time, fell in love. In the summer of 1978, they married on the porch of the family home. It was part of the July 4th celebration and many of their relatives had been able to attend. Matt and Melinda had carried on the tradition of opening the house to the community of Springfield. Mike could not help but remember the times of his youth on this very porch. He had never pretended to get married here, yet there he was, standing in the very place that he had dreamed of surfing at the beach. What else did life have in store for him?

The rest of college was hectic, juggling class and married life. Mike and Donna had part time jobs, but continued their friendship with John. Periodically, they would discuss their line-a-roller idea and how they really needed to figure out a way to actually patent, manufacture, and market the product.

After graduation, Mike went to work at a sporting goods store, and Donna found a job as a freelance artist. In 1980, Mike and John visited once again about their design. Mike asked his brother Jake to do some checking into the patent process and received some upsetting news. Two brothers from Minnesota, Scott and Brennan Olsen, had been working on a similar project. The Olsen brothers had already filed a patent application for a product they called a rollerblade. Mike and John were disappointed, but they were not defeated. They had formed a bond that they wanted to use in the future. They would try again with other types of sporting goods equipment.

Each of the young men had promising futures. Mike had been promoted several times and was now the manager of his store. He loved all sporting gear: the equipment, the clothing, the instructional classes that were offered, all of it. He was friends with most of the representatives from the product lines that his store carried and he was constantly brainstorming with them about ways to improve and enhance their lines of merchandise. John was employed with a marketing firm and when they would meet for a lunch, they would compare notes about their jobs. They would always part with a handshake, determined that someday they would partner and form a business together.

CHAPTER 24
MIKE AND DONNA

The home with the porch had continued to stay in the family. Jake had never married and had lived in the house with Matt and Melinda after law school. After he established his law practice in Springfield, his life had become more hectic and he was ready for a place of his own. When Mike and Donna married, Jake moved out and offered his room to them. He knew that the rooms needed to be filled with laughter and hopefully a few children. There had almost always been a child to play on the porch and too many years had gone by without that happening.

Donna, Mike's wife had always wanted to travel and with her artist degree, desired to visit every famous museum that they could. She had studied art, sculptures, and design history. Donna was always sketching ideas and taking notes. She was a good companion for Mike. With her creative eye and his quest for adventure they had daydreamed constantly of things that they could create. During one of the Fourth of July reunions, Mike

The Porch

had spent time showing Donna all of the sketchings that he had done when he was younger. She had been especially interested in the drawings that he had done of the house. They decided that it was time to suggest doing some repairing of the old house and the porch. Donna was all ready to design new flowerbeds and suggest redecorating ideas for the house.

The house was eighty-five years old and needed help. One night at dinner, it had been a rare occasion when the four of them were all seated together. Mike and Donna had some money that they were willing to put into the house in order to do some major renovating. They approached the conversation carefully. "Dad, what would you and mom think about the four of us working on a remodel and update of the house? We have some extra money that we would like to invest in it. We know that Archie and Jewell would have wanted us to respect the integrity of the basic design, yet we could do some major repairs." The four of them had talked for hours, working out the lists of things that needed to be done and things that they would have to put on a wish list.

They started on the outside while the weather was nice and continued on the inside when the weather turned cool. They hired a contractor to oversee the major projects such as a new roof and siding. The concrete walk was replaced. It had settled and had cracks that were large enough to lose a small child in. Fill dirt was brought in to level the yard and a lot of the old, overgrown shrubbery was removed and replaced. The garage needed new doors and Donna and Melinda were thrilled to have garage door openers installed.

They decided to have all of the windows replaced in order to make the house warmer in the winter. After a fresh coat of paint on the house and the porch, they all agreed that the house looked a lot like Mike's drawings that were fifteen or more years old. The inside did not take as much work. They spent their free weekends, wallpapering, painting, and cleaning the old, hardwood floors. It was hard work, but the four of them had been a great team and had wonderful memories of the project.

The remodeling had been lots of fun, but as the four of them had worked together, the conversations had frequently focused on Matt and Melinda's retirement and Mike and Donna's plans for starting a family. Matt and Melinda had decided that it was time to move on to a dream that they had shared for years. Matt was still flying commercially on a part-time basis and Melinda had trained two new women to take over her bookkeeping accounts where she worked. They had always wanted to travel and the time seemed right. They purchased a small condominium that they could call home when they were in Springfield and the rest of the time; they lived out of suitcases in exotic places around the world.

With Jake's help, Mike and John formed a partnership. They would design, develop, and market sporting goods equipment just like they had always planned. Their college plans were becoming a reality and their future looked bright.

Donna was working for a major advertising firm, so they knew that they would have excellent promotion for their products. In her free time, she would help Mary

The Porch

with advertising for the dealership. There was always the possibility that one day, when Mary was ready to retire; Donna could take over the management of the Ford dealership.

Before long, they were rocking a new baby on the front porch. A beautiful son was born to them in the spring of 1981. Soon to follow was another son and Donna found herself surrounded by males. Mike was quick to teach them all of the fun things to do outside and shared countless stories of his memories playing on the porch and in the front yard with Brandon. Donna traveled a lot with her job and was always glad when she returned home to find that the boys had had so much fun with their father. Mike and John had been able to work from their homes and had traveled when they needed to meet with clients. Mike had been home almost every afternoon when Barry and Sam came home from school.

Their first son, Barry, was a sports fanatic. He had always been an athlete. Since that first Christmas when there was a small football in his stocking and he said, "Ball," Mike hoped that he would be an outdoors kind of kid. The neighborhood kids had always gathered at their yard to choose up teams and play all types of sports. Mike was jokingly referred to as "Mr. Mom." He loved to be outdoors with the boys and enjoyed having the neighbors' children join in on every game that they played. He tried to teach all of the neighborhood children and especially his own sons, the importance of good sportsmanship and fair play.

Sam was the younger of the two boys. He was into running. The family had joked that it was because he had teased his big brother so often, that he had to learn how to run fast so that he could make a quick get-away. He decided early on that he was not into contact sports because he did not like to get knocked down. He was tall, thin, and agile and could run for long distances. He loved the feel of the wind on his face, as he would head down and around the Town Square for his mile run each afternoon, after school.

CHAPTER 25
TEN-YEAR-OLD BARRY-1991

"Barry is engrossed in mapping out football formations as Uncle Jake arrives for dinner"

Uncle Jake had pulled his Ford van up to the curb in front of the house. Jake had done the mental math as he calculated how old the house was. 1991 take away 1895 equaled ninety-six years old. He loved this old house and took advantage of visiting every chance that he could. Donna, his sister-in-law, had invited him for dinner with the family and he had been so busy gathering his paperwork from the front seat that he had not noticed Barry lying on his stomach, on the front porch. He swiveled his driver's seat to the right so that he could scoot into the seat of his wheelchair that was positioned behind the passenger's seat. Once Jake was secured in the chair, he opened the side panel of the van and engaged the power lift that lowered him to the ramp on the sidewalk.

Barry had realized that Jake was there and had run out to the van and offered to help. "Uncle Jake, you should have tapped the horn and I would have helped you sooner."

Jake replied and said, "I do this so often that I forget to let anyone help me. I'll let you get my folders off of the front seat. I've been to a very interesting meeting today at lunchtime and I have some things that I want to show the family. What is your mother fixing for dinner? I sure hope that it is her fried chicken."

Barry laughed and agreed, "I could eat mom's fried chicken every meal. The smells that are coming from the kitchen make me think that we might get our wish."

Barry was a tall, slender young man. With dark, slightly wavy hair that was cut close to his head and deep blue eyes that appeared to be like deep wells on his face, he was already getting calls from girls that he didn't even know. It seemed as if life was too good to be true. He was good at sports, had a friendly personality, and tons of friends. Don't let all of that fool you; ten-year-old Barry remembered many times when things didn't always go his way. There was the time that he embarrassed himself at baseball practice. He got so nervous that he had wet himself standing at home plate waiting for the perfect ball. He had tried to shove the sand around with his foot in order to cover up the wetness, but he knew that some of the guys had seen. And then there was the time that he forgot to study for the States and Capitals test and made a grade in the fifties. He had folded his paper quickly, put it away, and vowed that from that point on, he would try to always be prepared both in school and out on the field. He was the type of child that could envision a situation before it would occur. He kept mental lists of things that he needed to do and most of the time was fairly organized.

Mike had pulled into the driveway about the time that Jake was maneuvering his wheelchair up the ramp onto the porch. He studied his brother and his son, who was being such a gentleman with his uncle. He saw that Barry had been drawing on the front porch before Jake had arrived and knew that the spiral notebook probably had some new football plays and formations. When friends weren't around, Barry was usually working in the notebook when he wasn't practicing on the field. The coach had depended on him to think on his feet and allowed Barry to call the plays in the huddle. Instead of running the plays in with alternating players or signaling from the sideline, Barry had learned to change the plays at just the right time in order to confuse the other team.

When Barry wasn't designing plays for football practice, he was doing one of two other things. On the porch, he would plug in the Tudor electric football game. He and one of his buddies could play for hours. Their voices could be heard a block away. They would arrange their teams, push the switch, and let the vibrations and magnetism begin. Barry hollered, "Run defense. Sack the quarterback. Not him, the quarterback. You dummy, you ran the wrong way."

His friend whooped and hollered. "Your guy is a dummy. Can't he do anything right? There goes my guy! Swing out, go right, Pass! Pass! Psych. He kept the ball. What a sneak. Psyched you out. Score!"

They would laugh at themselves and each other- they had no control of where the men would move-but it was so much fun.

The other pastime was football related also. For his birthday, he had received the new Joe Montana football cartridge. It was a one-player game, but he loved it. He could throw and run, score and celebrate all in the comfort of his living room. Barry was consumed with football.

As Mike got out of the car and headed into the house, he thought briefly about the different dreams that had been played out on the porch. Nursing, piloting, studying to be a lawyer, surfing (*Oh, Brandon, what fun we had*), and now football. Mike had known since an early age that Barry loved football more than all of the other sports combined. Barry wanted to play football every chance that he got and the coaches seemed to think that he had real potential. Playing outdoors and staying in good physical shape had always been a top priority. The family had enjoyed all types of sports throughout the years. Sam ran track at school and with the YMCA, and Barry had played soccer, baseball, and now in the fourth grade, football.

CHAPTER 26
JAKE'S ACCOMPLISHMENTS

Their laughter had spilled into the house and continued throughout the meal. Sam had come in from his run just in time to wash up and grab his spot at the table. Donna loved these meals with her family. Barry and Sam had grown up quickly and because she and Mike took turns traveling with their jobs, it was not very often that they were all at the table together. After the two boys talked about their school activities, Uncle Jake had started talking about his meeting that he had been to at noontime.

"I have exciting news tonight. I went to a Rotary Club meeting today. I have been chosen, unanimously, to be a delegate and spokesperson at the International Convention of the Rotary Club.. The meeting will be in Mexico City, Mexico."."

"That is wonderful, Jake!" exclaimed Mike.

Barry, eyes full of admiration and pride shouted, "Way to go Uncle Jake!"

The Porch

Sam's words tumbled onto Barry's as he whooped and exclaimed. "Cool. Way Cool!"

When the ruckus died down, Donna tapped her glass with her spoon and said, "Let's all raise our glasses and make a toast to Jake." She gave them time put their forks down and raise their tea glasses. "Jake, we are so very proud of you and your perseverance. You never cease to amaze us with your drive and your desire to help others. So many would wallow in self-pity, yet you always want to use the blessings that you have in your life to do good for us, your friends, and people that you have yet to meet. We raise our glasses in honor of you this evening!"

They clinked their glasses together, and as they continued their meal, Mike asked for more details.

"Not that you don't deserve it, but how did that work out?"

"Well," answered Jake, "Apparently, I am the only one of the local membership that has been physically affected by polio and they decided that I would be the best delegate this year. The PolioPlus program was established in 1985 and their goal is to immunize children all over the world. There will be committee meetings about this program that they would like for me to participate in. Hopefully, in the future, polio will be eradicated around the world!"

The Rotary Club International had been in existence since 1905. A Chicago attorney by the name of Paul P. Harris, with three of his friends had chosen the name because they rotated the meeting to each members' office weekly. From early on, their goals had included encouragement and worthy enterprise for all types of businesses and businessmen. The service club had grown quickly and eventually became a worldwide association. Jake had been involved with the Rotary Club in Springfield ever since he had first established his law practice. He had researched and studied so much of what the Rotarians stood for and was ready to be a spokesperson for the polio cause. The fundraising had already begun and there was a potential for millions of dollars to be poured into the efforts. That and the volunteer man-hours that had been committed to were so exciting for Jake. In his wildest dreams, as he had read and pretended on the porch, he had never expected that he would have found a more useful cause for his talents.

Jake had accomplished other achievements throughout his life as well. After he had finished law school and set up his practice in Springfield, he had spent a lot of time working towards legislation that would help disabled persons. He was very fortunate, that in Springfield, many knew him and his history. When he met friends and acquaintances for a meeting or a meal, people were eager to help him with his wheelchair. This was not the case for many other Americans. There was a need for people with all types of limitations, to have access to restrooms, multi-storied buildings, transportation, employment, and communication, to name just a few. Jake had been working closely with congressmen from their state and others. Their hard work had paid off and many Americans would be able to function easier in society. President George

The Porch

H.W. Bush had signed into law, the Americans with Disabilities Act of 1990.

He had also worked on big plans for the house with the porch. Anticipating the upcoming one-hundred-year anniversary of the house, Jake had handled all of the necessary paperwork needed to register the residence for an historical marker. After contacting the National Register and filing the necessary paperwork, Jake had acquired a plaque for the front of the house. There had been criteria to meet and questions to address, but it had been worth the work. The plaque had been erected and the family had had a celebration to commemorate the occasion. The event had been phenomenal. The family had grown so quickly and the cousins, aunts, and uncles had had such a good time reminiscing about the history of the house and all of the loved ones that had lived there. Including the Fourth of July reunions, weddings, fellowships, and the recognition of being a historic part of America, the house with the porch was not a stranger to celebrating. Archibald and his wife Jewell would have been very, very proud.

CHAPTER 27
GAME CHANGER

Barry did well with his sports career throughout middle school and high school. He was agile on his feet and quick with his mind. The coaches liked his easy disposition and the fact that he was such a good role model and leader. Because of these factors, Barry had played on the Varsity team since the tenth grade. The family had become totally immersed in the Friday night game ritual and all of the aspects of football in a small town. Mike was active with the Booster's Club and when Donna was in town and able, she helped with fundraisers and bake sales. Barry's younger brother, Sam, was athletic as well, but his interests dealt with track and field. Just like Barry, he was light and quick on his feet and loved the exhilaration of feeling the wind on his face as he raced for the finish line.

The year was 1997, it was Barry's senior year, and he was the starting quarterback. It was the most important game of the season because they were playing the number one team in the district and this game could land them a spot in the playoffs. It had rained steadily for most of the first half and the field looked like a swamp. Both teams had slipped around and made terrible mistakes throughout the game. The buzzer for the two-minute warning signaled that it is was almost half time and the band and flag corps were on the sideline getting ready. Barry's team had the ball, it was snapped and as he went back for a pass, he slipped and fell. At the same moment, he got slammed by one of the defensive tackles. He immediately felt the pain – it was excruciating. There was a hush across the stands as the team doctor rushed to see about him. He signaled that they needed a paramedic and the ambulance that was standing by made its way around the track to be as close as possible to where Barry was laying. Mike, Donna, and Sam raced from the bleachers as quickly as possible and Cynthia, Barry's girlfriend, dropped her flag and rushed over to where the family had gathered.

The doctor told them, "He's breathing, just had the breath knocked out of him, but his leg is messed up pretty bad."

Mike impatiently responded, "Let's get him out of this mud and on to the hospital."

As Barry was loaded onto the stretcher and into the back of the ambulance, he gave a victory sign to the team and the fans that were nervously waiting to see if he was all right. The family agreed to meet at the hospital and Mike was allowed to ride along in the ambulance. Cynthia got permission from her sponsor to leave and the other flag members scrambled to readjust their routine.

Barry prayed silently on the way to the hospital as Mike tried to keep him alert and keep his mind off of his pain. "Son, I remember how bad my arm hurt when I broke it, but we'll get you fixed up in no time. Try to think about something else, get your mind off of how bad you're hurting. You didn't do anything wrong. You were playing a great game. Just remember, your mom and I love you."

Barry mumbled a, "Thank you, Dad," and as he drifted in and out of consciousness, he had a feeling deep in his heart that the last play of the first half would be the last play of his football career. All of his dreams and plans had been dashed in a split second of life.

Barry had grown up learning and knowing about lessons in life and how even the hard ones that brought such great disappointments could work out in ways that one might not even imagine. As he tried to take his mind off of the terrible pain that was shooting through his leg, he wondered about the dreams he had about being a college athlete and maybe even a pro. Why had those dreams been so vivid if they were not meant to be a part of his future? The pain medication that they had given him was beginning to take effect and as he had grown sleepy, he had thought that maybe, he would wake up and realize that this had all been a bad dream.

Days later, as Barry had become more alert, he had learned the future of his leg. The compound fracture would require more surgery and months of rehab. He would be able to walk again, but the promise of being able to play football was not mentioned. The days of hoping that he would awaken from this bad dream were over and the reality of what had happened had settled in.

Some of Barry's teammates had stopped by to visit and had brought sacks full of get well cards and messages from all of the kids at school. Barry asked about the team films. "Have you guys watched the clips from the game? Was it a late hit? What went wrong?

Several of his closest friends tried to cheer him up by telling him, "It was really just an accident, nothing to blame but the mud. Accidents just happen sometimes."

As long as they were there, Barry played along, chatting about his future and how quickly he planned on getting back on his feet, back to school, and back to the team.

After the jokes and the farewells, the room was empty for the first time since he had felt like dealing with the reality of it all. Up until now, Barry had had someone with him and he had not had much time to think on his own. It all began to settle in; how different his life was going to be and how much strength he would have to muster in order to make it through the next several months. He began to cry and wondered why did bad things happen to good people? He was too tired to even think about the future. He thought that he had it all planned out and now what? He fell asleep feeling very helpless and scared.

Barry awakened to find Cynthia sitting by the bed. She had been so sweet, to be waiting whenever she could, by his side. It had not been easy for her either. At school, everyone wanted new information about Barry and, at home, her family was hoping that this unfortunate accident would not affect her future. They knew that she'd always wanted to go to college to be a teacher and now they were afraid that she wouldn't pursue her dreams. They loved Barry like a son, but if his plans for college changed, they did not want Cynthia to alter her plans.

It was the first opportunity that she and Barry had had to be alone since the accident and there was awkwardness to their conversation. They began with niceties about family stuff and the friends at school and then they began to talk about their relationship. Cynthia had always been a good listener and knew so many of Barry's dreams and desires. He told her all about his fears and anger and the uncertainty about his future. "Cynthia, this is not what I thought we would be doing for the rest of our senior year. I wanted to win district, hold up a huge trophy, and meet with scouts about where I want to go to college. This is supposed to my time and now I am just laying here wondering when my next therapy session will be. I wanted to take you to prom and show you off and now you have to help me hobble down the hall with crutches."

Cynthia wanted to tell him how lucky he was to be hobbling with crutches and to stop feeling sorry for himself, but she answered by saying, " Barry, you know as well as I do that we don't get to plan the way life is going to lead us. You are still very fortunate that you are doing so well. I want us to still be able to go to prom and finish out our senior year."

Barry had been trying to figure out how he wanted to say something that he knew would upset her. "Just think before you answer, but I want you to think about dating other people. We had big plans for college and the future, but I don't want to be the one to hold you back. I have no way of knowing how much my leg is going to limit my life and my future activities and career."

She sucked in air, surprised by what Barry was suggesting. She quickly recovered and replied, "Don't be ridiculous! I want to help you. I want to be with you. Can't we just wait and discuss this some other time?" There was awkwardness in the room as they silently agreed to think and talk later.

On her way home, she stopped off to visit with her dad where he worked. He was honest with her as they talked about the obstacles that she might face as a result of Barry's injury. Her dad mentioned the depression that was sometimes a result of an accident and the frustration that Barry might feel throughout his rehabilitation. They also discussed the fact that Barry would probably not be recruited to play college ball. He repeatedly told her how much he loved Barry and wanted only the best for him, but that he also wanted only the best for her as well. . Back in her car, Cynthia cried for what seemed like eternity and realized that she truly loved Barry and could not imagine life without him. She willed herself to be strong enough to be by his side no matter what might happen.

Barry had been through another surgery and months of rehab and was able to go to prom and graduate with his class in May. He relied on crutches to keep himself from falling and injuring his leg again.

Cynthia was graduating as well and the families had gotten together at Barry's house for a celebration. There was enough food to feed a small army and people from far and wide had stopped by to congratulate them both. The porch had been decorated and there were as many people on the porch as there were in the house. Barry sat in a rocking chair and greeted people that were coming by to say congratulations and wish him well. College plans had changed quite a bit. Barry and Cynthia had agreed that they would each live at their own homes and attend the community college that was about thirty minutes away. Cynthia would drive Barry whenever he needed to go to rehab and they would wait for each other to study on campus and go to class.

Uncle Jake had come by to celebrate with Barry and the family. He, of all people, understood all of the emotions that Barry had been facing. Earlier that spring, he had shared with Barry how he had faced frustration in every day tasks that others took for granted and some of the ways that he had learned to compensate for them. The ramp had sure come in handy and one of the times that they had been visiting together, alone on the porch; Barry had told Jake about the times that he had thought about the ramp. When he was younger, he had wondered how different it would be for a person to not be able to do simple activities such as walking up and down the stairs.

Jake had let Barry talk through all of his emotions, knowing that Barry would probably not have to spend his entire life in a wheelchair. They had had great conversations about disabilities and how many differences there were now; compared to when Jake had been eighteen. Barry had remembered that Jake had worked on several pieces of legislation for the Disabilities Act. There was a new appreciation for all that Jake had been through. Since the accident, Jake and Barry had shared a new bond, one that would last a long time. Recently, Barry had been a lot more interested in his Uncle Jake and his activities with the Rotary Club.

The coaches from Barry's high school had come by the hospital on many occasions, to give Barry moral support. One of the coaches that he had really respected suggested that Barry think about an education degree so that he could become a coach. Barry had always been so adept at football and loved the game so much. Eventually, that had become part of his plan and as he and Cynthia had planned their future together; it had become a little easier to see how things were going to work out.

CHAPTER 28
THE WEDDING

There was another wedding on the porch. Cynthia and Barry became husband and wife on what had always been a special holiday. Barry had progressed with his therapy and was able to walk with the use of a cane. They had plans to live in the house with Mike and Donna. Sam was off to college on a track scholarship and there was an extra room for them. The year was 1999 and they had only been in college for a year. They spent more time together than apart and had quickly realized that they wanted to be married. The porch had seemed to be the perfect place for a summer wedding as it had for others in the past. Cynthia and Barry had spent countless hours on this porch and it only made sense that this was where they should begin their married life together. Barry had first seen Cynthia from this very place more than nine years before. He had been working on his football plays when she had roller-bladed by with her girlfriends. They were giggling and acting silly as they had called out to him. He had found out much later on that it had been Cynthia's idea to skate by his house and that she had had a crush on him for months. At the age of ten, he had not been at all interested in girls and remembered thinking that they were so dumb. Who would have guessed that this would have worked out this way?

The wedding was beautiful and all of the family was able to attend. They decided to have it on the July 4th weekend. They had a little break from their college classes and the family always had their reunion on the Fourth of July. They agreed to put their wedding topper in the wooden box that held all of the other treasures from the past. They included a program from the wedding and a list of all that were able to attend.

As the family was shuffling through the pictures, papers, and stacks of certificates and awards, one by one, someone would pick up the Japanese puzzle box and fiddle with it for a while. For obvious reasons, Barry was more interested in the Treasure Chests this year and spent some extra time looking at each item.

As he picked up the puzzle box, he commented, "This crazy box is still here, after all of these years. Does this fascinate anyone else as much as it does me? Maybe it's because my mind is always configuring diagrams and plays for football, but there has got to be a way to get this thing opened."

Cynthia asked, "What is the history of that box and why is it so hard to open?

"My great-great-grandfather put this in here, years ago. Every year, he would watch the family members pick it up, and try to open it. It has been told, that he always wore a mysterious smile on his lips and a mischievous glint in his eyes because he had a secret that no one else knew." Barry continued his story, "When he died, he took his mystery with him, and ever since then, we laugh and wonder if he is still getting pleasure from our futile attempts to open it."

Cynthia chuckled, "It reminds me of those Rubik's cubes that we played with growing up. I was pretty good with those. Now that I am a part of this family, I consider that a challenge that I want to tackle."

"Hey, you leave that tackling business up to me," Barry teased as he hugged his new bride.

It was not long before Cynthia was rocking a newborn on the porch. It was one of the first warm days in April and she was taking full advantage of the warm sunshine that was streaming onto the porch. Natalie looked so much like the pictures of the babies in Barry's family. She had Mike's fair skin and strawberry blonde hair and the deep blue eyes that were predominate in both of their families. She had Cynthia's small petite nose and perfectly shaped lips that parted as if she had something important to say.

Cynthia's days were full of caring for the baby, all of the wash and the errands. Donna still traveled a lot with her job, so Cynthia took care of meals and keeping the house while Mike worked or traveled with Donna. Barry had rehabbed to the point where he was able to drive, so he continued going to college. When they realized that they were going to have a baby, Cynthia had decided to take a semester off from school and would then return the next fall.

The Porch

Natalie was such a good baby and Cynthia found that she had free time to do more around the house than just cooking and cleaning. For years, Mike had been working on the family history and his excitement about it had begun to interest Cynthia. She took advantage of her free time to organize old photos and newspaper clippings. They assembled scrapbooks and updated the journals that had been stored for years in the Treasure Chests. She hoped to have a lot of it finished for the next Fourth of July reunion. Before she and Barry had married, she had enjoyed celebrating the Fourth with his family. She thought that it was a terrific idea that great-great-grandfather Archibald had initiated many years before. His vision of storing all of the keepsakes in the crates under the porch and making it one of the focal parts of the Fourth of July had kept the family aware of their rich heritage. The name, Treasure Chests, kept the younger children in the family interested as well. It was always so cute, what the youngest would bring to put into them each year. As the children matured throughout the years, you could watch them look for their own memorabilia each time that it was displayed.

CHAPTER 29
THE FOURTH OF JULY 2003

The year was 2003 and the family had their annual reunion and Fourth of July party on the porch. They celebrated Cynthia's graduation from college along with a baby shower for Sam and his wife. Cynthia had been able to make up for the semester that she had missed when Natalie was born and she and Barry were now finished with their education degrees. Barry was going to be a coach at Springfield High School. It had been hard at first to go out on the field where he had had his life-changing accident. He had done his student teaching there and the students had seemed to have such a huge amount of respect for him. After graduation, there had been an opening for an offensive coach and Barry had seemed perfect for the job. Cynthia had always loved her fifth grade teacher and thought that that would be her favorite grade to teach. After doing her student teaching in the third grade, she had changed her mind. When there were new openings for the fall, she was hired to teach third grade.

The Porch

Lots of new memorabilia was added to the Treasure Chests. Aunt Mary had passed away and they placed the obituary, a program from the funeral and some pictures from her photo albums in it. The church had been overflowing with friends and family. Mary had done a terrific job of handling the dealership and the town of Springfield had honored her in a memorable show of affection.

Natalie had picked some of her favorite artwork from preschool and her daddy had helped her to put it into a folder with her picture on the front. She was learning her letters and had tried to write her name on each picture.

At the age of three, Natalie was a beautiful little girl. Her hair had changed color a bit and in the sunlight, it had several colors of red and auburn. Her face had a more mature look; yet her eyes and mouth had remained serious. She was a quiet child and liked to play by herself. She went to a daycare that the school district provided for parents that worked in the school system. Her teacher said that she was bright, but preferred activities that were away from the large group. Her favorite center was the housekeeping center where she was always making sure that all of the dolls were clothed and well fed. She seemed to have such motherly instincts.

Natalie loved the afternoons when Granddaddy Mike picked her up early so that she could go home and play by herself. He sometimes treated her to ice cream or would let her choose a small toy at the store. Mike loved to sit on the porch and watch her eat her ice cream. She was so dainty and meticulous as she licked around the sides and was so careful not to drip a single drop. The sunlight would catch the redness of her hair and her eyes twinkled with excitement as she enjoyed her special time with her grandfather.

"Granddaddy, I love you."

"I love you too, Natalie."

After raising two boys, Mike had been mystified that a little girl could bring him so much joy. She loved to hear him tell stories about this porch and how he used to play in this very spot where they were sitting.

"Tell me another story granddaddy."

"Which one would you like to hear?"

"Tell me the one about you and Brandon when you skateboarded down Uncle Jake's ramp, down the sidewalk, bumped over the curb, and ended out in the street."

Mike reminisced in silence for a moment before he began. "Oh, that one sounds funny now, but at the time it was very scary. We were both racing down the ramp at the same time and were so intent on trying to beat each other that we forgot to watch for cars. Thank goodness the driver was watching us, because he was able to stop his car about the time we went flying into the street."

Natalie took the stories very seriously and asked, "Did you get into trouble?"

"Well, I didn't tell my parents, but Brandon did and when my mom heard it from her sister, Brandon's mom, I got in more trouble than if I had told the truth in the first place."

"What happened to you?" Natalie asked.

Mike replied, "I got spanked with my dad's belt."

Natalie's eyes were as large as saucers as she tried to imagine being spanked at all, least wise with a belt. "Oh, I have never been paddled like that."

Mike was going to take full advantage of the moment to make a big impression on her. "I hope that you never do anything like that; it is not good to keep secrets from your mom and dad. They love you very much and want what is best for you."

CHAPTER 30
THE MYSTERY UNFOLDS—2010

Mike had returned home to find Natalie, his precious, little red-haired granddaughter, playing dolls on the front porch. As usual, she was pretending that she was a nurse and he had a remembrance of stories that he had heard through the years about his grandmother, Sara. Natalie had shoulder length hair with reddish highlights. He watched as she continuously flipped the wisps of hair that fell onto her face as she concentrated on her pretend play. Her eyelashes were long and framed her beautiful, sparkling blue eyes. There were sprinkles of freckles on her cheekbones and a sweet smile as she murmured and tended to her patients. She was dressed in a pair of jeans and her shirttail was half tucked in and half out. She was wearing socks and her shoes were lying haphazardly on the porch. Mike wondered to himself, "Did she even go into the house when she raced home from school? Did she remember to finish her homework and eat a snack or did she drag out all of her dolls and take up playing where she left off last night?" He sometimes worried along with her mother and father that she was too focused on this idea of becoming a nurse; that the rest of her life was passing her by in a blur.

Matt and Melinda were on a safari in Africa and Mike and Donna had been gone more than they had been home. They had suggested several years ago that Barry and Cynthia fix the house up for their family and have Mike and Donna stay in the extra, upstairs bedroom when they were home. Barry argued at first, because it was Mike's house, but Donna was quick to point out that the house had been many things for many families, but it had not really ever belonged to one person. She knew that she and Mike still had so many adventures that they wanted to experience and Sam was now married with a family. He and his wife had moved to a new housing development in Springfield after college and Sam was managing the family Ford dealership. Barry and Cynthia had consented and had remodeled the master bedroom for themselves. They had paid a contractor to enlarge their closet, paint a new color scheme, and refinish the hardwood floors. Mike and Donna had admired the finished product and had secretly wished that they had done the work for themselves years before.

After Mike had returned from the antique dealer, he and the family were trying to figure out the reason for the numbers on the piece of paper that was found inside of the Japanese puzzle box. Mike had decided to look more carefully at the floor plans of the original house that Archie and Jewell had built. As he was studying later on that evening, he made a startling observation that he should have thought of long before. The original house was built with very small closets; at the time, it was a great idea to have a closet at all.

As he began to go through the different rooms, comparing them to the blueprints, he was careful to look at the faded notes that were on the plans. Something had been penciled in that was not a part of the original drawing. On the wall, in the corner of the master bedroom closet was a symbol that could possibly be where a safe was added. In Archie's handwriting was the date 1945. If his memory served him correctly, that was the year that the house had been fifty years old and had undergone some major remodeling. Thinking back to the recent remodeling that Barry and Cynthia had done, he did not remember seeing anything different about the interior wall of the closet. He wondered if that closet had been enlarged before, sometime in the past. He would have to wait for morning, when he could empty part of the closet and look carefully at the original wall. That was the bedroom that Cynthia and Barry were asleep in. He was beginning to formulate a reasonable solution in his mind and now thought he knew the answer to the mystery of the numbers.

CHAPTER 31
THE SAFE

"Upon opening the safe, Mike wonders how these papers and this box will change his family's life"

After a restless night, with many half-in-half-out sleepy dreams, Mike had been ready to tackle his project. He took time for a quick cup of coffee and laid the original plans of the house across the bed in the master bedroom. The family had been up for a while and were out the door to work and to school. Mike had asked their permission to look in their closet for some clues to the number mystery. Cynthia had been dying to stay home from work in order to help him, but she knew that at the last minute it would be hard to get a substitute for her classroom.

Mike quickly removed the clothes from the rack in the back part of the closet and laid them across the bed. He then began to feel around on the paneling in the location where he thought there might be a clue. *Bingo!* There was a section of paneling that was hinged in the corner, very much hidden by the trim. He grabbed a screwdriver and carefully pried the paneling open. He was surprised that no one had ever mentioned that this was here. Maybe no one had ever known. Leave it to Archie with all of his gadgets and innovations to have built a secret trapdoor in the wall.

He could hardly contain himself as he opened the paneling. A safe; now his hunch was correct about the mystery of the numbers. By now, he had memorized them and was ready to put them to use. This had to be the oldest safe that he had ever laid his eyes on. If the safe was added during the remodeling in 1945, then it was about 65 years old. He secretly prayed that the combination lock on the safe would not be too old and rusty, that the numbers would be correct, and that there would not be yet another puzzle to figure out.

He paused for a split second, wondering if he should wait for someone to come home and experience this with him. "No, I have to know now. Archie was such a character. He must have known what this moment would feel like to a person in a future generation.

What a feeling of exhilaration. When Archie put those numbers into that Japanese puzzle box he must have realized that it would lead to this suspenseful moment. What will I find? Would it lead to yet another mystery? Will I be rich? Will I be famous?"

Mike did love a mystery, but he was ready for some answers. He was fortunate enough to have had enough money to be comfortable and his comics and history of the old house were causing enough notoriety for now. What was he secretly hoping for?

He had carefully spun the dial several times to loosen it up. Surprisingly enough, the dial had moved quite easily. Mike tried to decide if he should start counterclockwise and then go right and left or clockwise and then go left and right. He had a 50/50 chance of getting it right on the first try. He decided to start by going to the right, stopping at the first number. He paused for a bit and remembered all of those times he had used the combination lock on his locker at school. He would get in such a rush and would have to start all over again. He turned the dial back to the left and paused again. There were three more numbers and then hopefully the safe would open. Back to the right; then to the left and finally back to the right. He held his breath and pulled the knob towards himself. It opened; the safe had actually opened. His heart pounded as if it would beat out of his chest.

He had another fleeting thought, *I have been writing about this quest and the mystery of the numbers in my comic strip. How will I put this into the story line if it is something monumental? If it is a treasure like you read about in the old novels, will my life and the lives of my family change forever?* He would worry about all of that later. Thank goodness, he had a flashlight handy. The inside of the safe was dark and rank. Mike had to back out and breathe some fresh air for a minute. "Wow, that is some nasty, old antique air." There were several bundles of papers folded neatly. He carefully lifted them out, hoping that they would not fall apart in his hands. There was also a small box, the type that you would give to someone with a ring inside.

He scooted some of the clothes over and sat carefully on the bed. He began to gently open the papers. Some were folded, some were flat, and some were rolled. The rubber bands had long ago dried and broken apart. He recognized some of the documents. They were apparently duplicates of some of the special things that Archie had put into the Treasure Chest. The picture of Henry Ford and Archibald when the dealership was opened way back when, a very yellowed picture from the newspaper when Archie and Jewell were married, and the original directions as to how to open the mystery box. Seeing the directions made him stop for a second and laugh. "I hope that somewhere, Archie is having a good laugh at my expense. These numbers of the combination of a hidden safe, in a box that couldn't be opened without the directions that were in the safe. What a character."

One of the flat documents looked unfamiliar. It looked like an old stock certificate. As he turned his body toward the window so that there would be some sunlight on the paper, it dawned on him that it was a stock certificate for one hundred shares of stock from the Ford Motor Company. Why would Archie have hidden this away, not knowing how many years it would be before someone would find it? He tried to think back about the stock market throughout the past one hundred years. There had been so many ups and downs in the market not to mention the stock market crash in 1929. The financial problems just this past year would have affected the value of one hundred shares. All of a sudden, he remembered that Archie had told the family that he was not one of the original investors and that common stock shares had not been available until 1956. This certificate was probably fifty-four years old. He looked again at the stock certificate, this time more closely. There it was, the date of issue, 1956. "Wow, an original, from the first year that stock was publicly traded!"

The major automobile companies had just begun to come out of the crisis they had faced and the bailout of 2009 was still fresh on people's minds. He also tried to remember what he had read about the Ford Motor Company. He didn't remember that they had needed any of the government bailout money. The dealership that Archie had started had stayed in the family through all of these years. In fact, Mike's other son Sam, was managing it now. It had been a rough couple of years. There had been lay-offs throughout the city and people had really gone through some rough times. Neighbors were having garage sales and were selling things that they no longer needed to get extra cash, and what had been a renowned dealership for miles in all directions, had become a dealership that had more used cars for sale than new ones. What had recently helped the most was the Cash-for-Clunkers program. Sam had taken in a record number of old cars and had been able to recover a lot of the government money in exchange for destroying the old gas-guzzlers that were sitting on his lot. Besides all of that, lately, he had sold a lot of new cars and it seemed to him, that the local economy was picking up a bit.

CHAPTER 32
THE RING

Mike had saved the small box for last. He did not know why, but he had not opened it yet. Something about the box made him wonder if there would be yet one more unanswered treasure. As he opened the box, he realized that in it was a very old ring. It appeared to be a man's ring. The band was worn and Mike knew that he was going to have to find the magnifying glass to read any inscriptions that it had on it. In the same box was a piece of folded paper. Maybe the clues to this mystery would be included. He decided to clean up the mess that he had made and spend some time at the kitchen table with the ring box. He opted to leave the clothes out of the closet so that he could show Cynthia, Barry, Natalie and Jason all about his treasure hunt. He was also going to take some pictures so that he would have something to use in his comic strip. Besides that, he wanted to document all of this for the Treasure Chests. What a story this would be for the next Fourth of July family celebration. What would relatives think fifty years from now? As a fleeting thought, Mike wondered, "Will there be any more mysteries for the future generations to try to unravel? This sense of excitement has kept this generation alive and maybe there needs to be some new adventure seeded so that there is something to look forward to."

As Mike sat down at the kitchen table, with a hot cup of coffee, he wondered about the ring. There had been very little jewelry that had been handed down in the family. Several of the women had left rings and bracelets for their daughters and granddaughters, but this was a man's ring. He had thought back to the men that had gone to college and what had happened to their class rings. He just had a funny feeling that this ring did not belong to anyone in their family. If so, he questioned, "What was Archie doing with it and why had he placed it in the safe?" As he softly rubbed around on the ring, pondering its mysteries, he noticed that it was a military ring. He could feel an engraving on the inside of the ring. Matt had been a pilot during WWII, but the ring was from the U.S. Military Academy at West Point and Matt had not been able to go there. Using the magnifying glass, he noticed the initials, T.W.K. and a worn date, 1941.

Mike gathered the notes that he and Cynthia had organized when they were working on the family history data. He read and reread and the only correlation that he could come up with was that his grandmother Sara had been a nurse during WWII. Her husband, Robert had died earlier in her life and the ring would probably have belonged to someone much younger than her.

The Porch

Mike had totally forgotten about the folded note that had been inside of the ring box. He had been so intent on trying to place the ownership of the ring to a family member. When he remembered the note, he opened the box, grabbed it, and unfolded it. At first, his eyes scanned the note. He did recognize the handwriting. It was grandmother's. She had also signed it. He had been correct about the time period, but what he read next, really blew his mind.

May 1952

Dear Loved One,

I do not know when or why you will be reading this note. When I was nursing the sick and injured soldiers in the Philippines, there was one soldier that became very dear to me. He reminded me so much of my precious son Matt. I could only imagine how frightening it must have been to be injured so badly and to know that he was probably going to die without any loved ones around. I would pray with him and listen to him tell me about his son that was back at home with his sister. His wife had died during childbirth and he was so afraid of what would happen to his son after he died. He asked me to try to get in touch with his sister whenever I returned home. I tried for many years to no avail, and now, if you are able, please try to piece

together this missing link. If you are able to find him, please tell him how much his father loved him and how brave he was even in his death. His name was Thomas Wayne Kirkland. The son's name was Tommy Jr. I have locked this ring away with some of my father's precious papers. Thank you for all of your help.
   God Bless You,

Love,
Sara

Mike leaned back in the chair, exhausted. His mind had been able to visualize the events that had been briefly described in the note. Sara, a loving and caring nurse, cared for hundreds of hurt and maimed soldiers. She missed her own children so much, yet knew that she had a purpose to minister and care for so many that died. Sara had tried everything that she could have done to locate the soldier's son. She felt the disappointment and frustration that her life had ended without completing her mission. He knew from the records, that his grandmother had died early from health complications as a result of the war. This note must have been written just before she got sick and passed on.

He carefully folded the note and placed it and the ring back in the box. "Wow!" The adrenaline rush that he had felt as he opened the safe had now become a feeling of uncertainty. This would be a project that he could let Natalie help with. She had felt let out that she had not been with him at the antique dealer the day that he learned how to open the puzzle box. Now, she would be disappointed that she wasn't there when he found the safe. She loved to do research on the computer, so with some adult supervision, he could let her try to trace the whereabouts of Tommy Jr. Kirkland. There was so much to think about and he couldn't wait for the family to come home.

CHAPTER 33
THE FOURTH OF JULY 2010

The economy of 2009 had been the worst since the Great Depression. After a beautiful prayer about the abundance of blessings that this family had had in spite of hard times, the family had enjoyed a spread to beat all. Just about everyone in the entire family had come to this reunion because they knew that Mike had important news for the family. Cynthia had sent out beautiful invitations that had a mysterious flair and no one wanted to miss this Fourth of July, 2010. The house, the hotel, and the two motels in town were full of overnight guests. In all they had counted forty-three loved ones. Mike was now fifty-five years old and he hoped that he would have many more of these wonderful get-togethers. As they ate and visited, many talked about the previous year. The Swine Flu had been quite a scare in the spring of 2009 and then tapered off for a while. In the fall of the year, there had been quite a frenzy with young and old alike deciding on which shots and how many shots they should get. The economy had finally bottomed out and several in the family had lost their jobs and then had been fortunate to get new ones. The older relatives talked about the stories that were recorded about the Great Depression and how the two periods of history had compared.

There was also much discussion about President Obama and whether or not his presidency had been good for the country. The bailout programs and the healthcare issues were first and foremost on everybody's minds. They all wondered how taxes were going to be in the days to come and how the future generation would be paying for the economic crisis. The younger children finished their meals and ran out into the yard to play. Natalie was very interested in the conversations about the worldwide effect that the Swine Flu had had. She was even able to interject some conversation about a few cancer patients that she had read about that had died because their immune systems were too weak to combat the illness. The adults were always amazed that for such a young girl, Natalie was so confident and ready to achieve her goals. Even today, she chose to sit and visit with the adults instead of playing hide-and-seek with her cousins.

When the coffee was ready and the myriad of desserts was laid out on the kitchen table, everyone hit the buffet again. The children were ready for a break from their play, and before they had a chance to run off again, Mike decided that it was time to gather the entire brood on the porch. He had spent many hours deciding how he would reveal all of his findings. Because Cynthia had alluded to a mystery theme for the reunion, he decided to carry the idea into his presentation. He reenacted his discovery of the safe with a scavenger hunt. The Treasure Chests had been displayed on long tables in the living room and the server table in the dining room. He had noticed several of the more curious relatives picking through the memorabilia.

Throughout the day, several had pumped him for information. Questions such as, "What is this mysterious find that you are so secretive about?"

"We have been looking at all of these old keepsakes for years, what could we possibly be learning that's new?"

Mike had just smiled, knowing that when he revealed his great find, there would be even more questions.

The scavenger hunt began by dividing the family into five teams. The teams were large, but the younger children needed help with the clues and some of the older folks were willing to only observe. As it turned out, as time progressed, many of them joined in because the excitement was too much to endure from a lawn chair. Cynthia had helped Mike and together they had printed a list of places to go around the house to look for clues. The order was different on each list and the teams moved from one part of the house to another.

One group was in the living room looking for information in the old paperwork that was laid out in chronological order, while another group was in the dining room examining the original floor plans of the house. A third group was to stop and visit with Mike in order to hear the story about the Japanese puzzle box.

He made certain to keep his hands on it at all times. He had a sneaky suspicion that one of the kids might try to close it, thinking that he or she could get it open again. Mike was not taking any chances on that happening. A fourth group went upstairs and visited with Cynthia and Natalie about the ring box and a picture of the ring. They read and discussed the note that Sara had written so many years before. Another group met with Barry in the backyard. He had set up a display on the picnic table, showing all of the old paperwork that had been found in the safe. As he was making his presentation, he did not mention the safe or its location. Donna helped each group to stay on their route along with answering various questions.

After the groups made the rounds of the different stations, they were to huddle up and discuss all of the information among themselves. Then Cynthia handed them each an envelope with questions inside. As they read and reread the questions, several sent members of their team back to look again at the clues that were provided at the five stations. Some of the older relatives that had spent many years hearing the stories about Archie and looking through the keepsakes thought that they knew how the mystery was going to unfold, but they allowed the younger ones to search the information on their own. The questions seemed very simple, but that made it more fun for the younger children. As Mike, Donna, Barry, Cynthia, Natalie and Jason had developed the theme for the reunion; they had all agreed that many of the younger generation were not very interested in the Treasure Chests and all of the memorabilia. They were hopeful that by creating this game, relatives in the future would bring more mementos and keepsakes in order to keep the traditions alive.

The five questions that were in the envelope were printed on individual pieces of paper and were folded and numbered. They were instructed to read the questions in numerical order, following the directions on each one before opening the next one.

Question 1: Did you notice what was missing from the Treasure Chests?

Question 2: Did you figure out what the numbers in the Japanese puzzle box were for?

Question 3: Did you determine where Barry found all of the original papers.

Question 4: What would you say if you were able to find and meet the man whom the ring belongs to?

Question 5: When you visited with Barry did you notice the date on the Ford stock certificate?

As the groups finished going through their questions, they began to crowd around the floor plan drawings of the house. Some of the relatives began to search the house from floor to ceiling. Donna laughed and shouted for all to hear, "I'm certainly glad that we cleaned under the beds and all of the closets. You have looked in every nook and cranny of this old house."

The Porch

A group of the teenagers went down the steps under the front porch and carefully inspected the old ice cellar that had been converted into storage for the Treasure Chests. After a while, there came a shout from the master bedroom area. Adam, Sam's oldest son, had found the paneling where the trap door was concealed. Mike was secretly pleased that the person to find the safe was a teenager that might someday live in this house.

"I found something," Adam hollered. He was in the process of prying the paneling open when the rest of the family crowded into the bedroom. "Uncle Mike, bring me those numbers, I want to see if I can open this safe." Mike appeared and pressed his way through the eager spectators. They were all laughing and commenting that no one nowadays knew how to use a combination safe. Adam proudly boasted that it was probably the same as turning the lock on his bicycle lock and sure enough after a few tries; he was able to open the safe. Obviously, the safe was empty because Mike had pulled all of the papers out and gotten them ready for the reunion. While everyone was all together, Mike told the details about the night that he had figured out that there must have been a safe somewhere in the house. He went on to tell about the next morning when he had made the discovery and how thrilling it was to try to put all of the pieces of the puzzle together. He mentioned that he had written it all down so that it could be added to the journals that would go into the Treasure Chests.

As he began to tell the part about the small ring box, the family grew very quiet and pensive. Mike hoped that the drama around this afternoon would spark interest in the young people in the group. Sure enough, the room was so still that even a whisper did not break the silence. He told as much as he could about Sara and her time in the Philippines and then got to the part about the young man asking her to try to find his long, lost son. Mike helped the youngest family members with the math. "Let's assume that the baby was born about 1940. 2010 minus 1940 equals seventy. The son is not a boy at all. He is probably in his early seventies. He is only about fifteen years older than me." Mike also continued to share how distraught that Sara had been when she knew that her time was near and that she had failed to locate him. At this point, the room was feeling too crowded, and there was so much more to tell. Mike suggested that they all go back out to the porch and the front steps, so that everyone would have a place to sit and be more comfortable.

After everyone had time to refill their drinks and relocate, Mike asked Natalie to come and stand next to him. He placed his arm around her shoulder as he began, "You are all aware of how compassionate and caring that Natalie is. For such a young girl, she is quite sure of what she wants to be in life. Her parents, Donna and I, are very proud of how conscientious she is about her education. She is constantly searching the internet for new advances in the medical field, cancer research and nursing improvements. For all of these reasons, I asked her to be my assistant in trying to locate Mr. Kirkland. I have asked her to explain to you what all we have done in solving this part of the mystery."

Natalie began hesitantly, but quickly gained her confidence. "When granddaddy first showed me the ring and the letter about Mr. Kirkland, I felt a little overwhelmed. It had been such a long time, and we didn't have very much information. Little by little, we traced through ancestry websites and finally found three men that might have been the right Mr. Kirkland. We decided that it would be best to write some letters describing the information that we had. Within weeks, we had responses. One of the gentlemen that we had located was the right person. Mr. Thomas Wayne Kirkland, Jr. was still alive and invited us to come and visit. We set an appointment time, and Granddaddy and I headed out on a weekend road trip."

Natalie paused while many murmured their surprise about finding the man and their excitement about what happened next. She continued, "It was a memorable weekend. It took us about five hours to reach his city and along the way granddaddy, and I talked a lot about what we thought the visit would be like. We stopped to get a bite to eat and were then ready to go to his house. It seemed to take forever for someone to answer the door-we were afraid that he had forgotten that we were coming. A girl about my age opened the door, and after we introduced ourselves, Kelly invited us in. Mr. Kirkland was sitting at the kitchen table and invited us to join him. He had a cup of hot cocoa and Kelly offered us each a cup. The four of us sat and visited for a bit, granddaddy and I quickly realizing that Mr. Kirkland was blind."

Natalie paused again, taking a sip of her lemonade and allowing all of this information to sink in. She continued, "Kelly began to tell us about how she would come by after school and on the weekends to keep her grandfather company and make sure that he had some hot meals. It seems that all that he really knew about his father was that he was a pilot and had died during World War II. His aunt had not received any of his personal effects from the Army, and he didn't dream of ever knowing anything more.

We opened up the letter that Sara had written and asked Kelly if she would like to read it to him. She did, and there was not a dry eye around the table. Mr. Kirkland raised his face, hopefully expecting what would come next.

Granddaddy pulled out the ring box and placed it in his hands. He fumbled to get the box opened and then removed the ring, placing the box on the table. He felt all over the ring, outside and then the inscription on the inside. His face lit up like the fireworks on the Fourth of July! He was one of the happiest people that I have ever met. The rest of our visit was just as great.

Kelly and I had so much to talk about school and what we liked to do in our free time. They both kept telling us over and over again, how much this had meant to them. Granddaddy and I spent the entire trip coming home, telling and retelling each other, the story and how much fun that we had had.

The Porch

The family clapped and congratulated Natalie and Mike for a job well done. This was an exciting ending to a wonderful day.

As the family started to get up and move around, Sam, Barry's brother interrupted, "Hey, Dad, wait a minute. That's a great story, but we're not finished here. Am I the only person here that has remembered the Ford stock certificate?"

He glanced in Mike's direction, noticed Mike's grin and continued, "How did that stock get in the safe, and how much is it worth?"

Mike took center stage again and said, "You all might have to sit here a little longer. I was wondering if anyone was going to remember the stock. You noticed that the date on the stock was 1956. That means that that stock certificate has been in that safe for fifty-four years, and no one knew about it. It also means that Archie was ninety-one when he bought it and put it in the safe. That was the first year that Ford stock was publically traded, and it is also the same age that Archie was when he passed away. The only thing that we have been able to figure out is that when he realized that the stock was being offered, he went to the bank, purchased the stock, came home and placed it in the safe. How he did all of that without being noticed is beyond me. He was a clever man and he loved his surprises."

Mike took a break while everyone chuckled and speculated about the sequence of events and then he continued, "I asked a good friend of mine that knows a lot about the stock market, to trace the history of the Ford Motor Company Stock. The value of the stock might have split several times, dividends would have accrued and we are not sure what Archie originally paid for each of the one hundred shares. The original certificate is so old, that it is going to take a while to determine what *it* is worth and what will be the best thing for us as a family to do with it. I promise to consult with all of you when I find out some more information."

Several of the relatives made wise crack comments about making sure that they returned next year to find out how rich they had become. As the celebration was winding down, many of the family members had more questions for Natalie and Mike. After all seemed satisfied with the answers, Mike refilled his tea glass. He watched the different groups of relatives laughing and enjoying each other's company. Today of all days had been a very monumental day for him and all of the others. He thought of the ancestors that would have loved to have been here, especially Archie.

Mike knew that the legacy of the house, the Treasure Chests, and the porch would continue on with this family. His heart was full of joy and he could not wait to add this chapter of the family's history to the journals and to his comic strip series.

CHAPTER 34
SPRINGFIELD

It was time to head on down to the Town Square. The festivities would be in full swing and they wanted to find the best spots for their lawn chairs. They packed up leftovers to take for a snack supper. They could hear the music from the gazebo as the bands were taking turns with the entertainment. The midway rides and arcades had been set up for several days and the booths with food and crafts were teeming with good things to eat and gifts to buy. The fireworks show would begin at dark, so there were several hours to walk around, take in the livestock show or a tractor pull, spend money, and eat really greasy snacks. The kids were all begging money from their parents and running off to join the fun.

Mike and Donna, along with several others, stayed at the house just long enough to move everything from the yard into the house. The porch was cleaned up and once everything was in place, they walked to the square to join the others. Mike and Donna held hands as they strolled along and reminisced about what a wonderful day that it had been.

Donna asked Mike a question that he had already had in his mind for days. "How will we ever again have an exciting Fourth of July like we have had this year?"

Mike smiled a sly grin and replied, "I have been thinking about that very thing and have already planned on placing a few special surprises in the Treasure Chests. I want to keep the history of this old house and the legacy of this porch alive for many years to come."

Donna grinned and found herself already looking forward to the next summer.

Mike wondered out loud, "Who do you think will be the next ten-year-old to play on the porch?

CPSIA information can be obtained
at www.ICGtesting.com
Printed in the USA
LVOW04s1405251016
510206LV00011B/152/P